PUFFIN BOOKS

THE RED WIND
The Kingdom of the Lost

When a devastating red wind sweeps across the land,
brothers Bily and Zluty are forced to fight for their
survival and journey into the perilous unknown.

A magical new series for younger readers from
the award-winning author of *Little Fur*.

PUFFIN BOOKS

Published by the Penguin Group
Melbourne • London • New York • Toronto • Dublin
New Delhi • Auckland • Johannesburg • Beijing
Penguin Books Ltd, Registered Offices: 80 Strand, London WC2R 0RL, England
Published by Penguin Group (Australia), 2011
Text and illustrations copyright © Isobelle Carmody, 2010
The moral right of the author/illustrator has been asserted. All rights reserved.
Cover and internal design by Marina Messiha
Printed and bound in Australia by Griffin Press
National Library of Australia Cataloguing-in-Publication data available.
ISBN 978 0 14 330686 3
puffin.com.au

MIX
Paper from
responsible sources
FSC® C009448

ISOBELLE CARMODY

THE RED WIND

The Kingdom of the Lost

BOOK 1

PUFFIN BOOKS

To Adelaide,
for whom Zluty and Bily came to life

one

STONEFALL

1

Once there lived two brothers in a cottage in the middle of a vast bare plain. Their names were Zluty and Bily. Both brothers had the same grey eyes and pink cheeks, the same small black noses and round ears with just a hint of pointiness in them. But Zluty's fur was yellow, and Bily's was white and soft and his tail was longer.

Bily was rather timid. He was also patient and very good at coaxing to life the seeds brought to him from afar by his bird friends. He spent each afternoon in the vivid garden he had wooed from the hard stony earth of the plain. As well as a wild

confusion of flowers, there were many bushes
and plants that produced fruit or vegetables. Bily
would gather these and make delicious jams and
preserves and sauces, or he would dry them. These
were important to the brothers, for Winter on the
plain was long and harsh and nothing grew.

Bily loved his garden and he loved cooking but most of all he loved the sturdy cottage that he and Zluty had built. Its walls were made from stones of various colours and sizes gathered from the plain. Its roof was made of tough grass woven into tiles laid over thick pieces of wood. The tiles were bound together so that they fitted tightly against one another, and on the rare occasions when it rained not a single drop leaked through. Inside the hut was the small stone oven where Bily baked bread and pies. In Winter he and Zluty would sit close to its open mouth and warm their toes and fingers while the icy winds blew outside. Bily loved the oven and his small bed in its nook by the window, and the wooden table and two chairs that Zluty had made for them to sit on when they ate. But best of all he loved the big cave under the cottage, which served as a cellar.

Here, all the pots of preserves and jams and chutneys he made in Summer and Autumn stood in rows alongside urns of honey, bales of sweet-grass, woven sacks of grain and rice and flour, and great mounds of ground cones. There were two neat doors in the floor of the cottage that opened to reveal the steps they had dug down to the cellar.

There was a second entrance outside the cottage, with a ladder, but they usually only used this for big or dirty things that could not be brought through the cottage.

Bily sometimes went down to the cellar just to look at everything that he and Zluty had so carefully prepared for the Winter to come, and to admire his store of seeds and bulbs. Occasionally, he would open the stopper of one of the urns of honey, or the smaller jugs of tree sap, and smell the richness that flowed out into the air. Then he would press the stopper back into its place and give a great sigh of pleasure at how wonderfully safe it all made him feel.

Zluty also cherished their cottage and its well-stocked cellar, but what he loved most was to think about the immense and mysterious forest that grew at the northern edge of the world.

Bily had never been to the Northern Forest, but Zluty made one long journey there each Autumn to gather mushrooms and tree sap and honey. It took four days for him to reach the edge of the forest, two days to forage, and four days to return. Zluty knew his brother worried about him the whole ten days he was away. No tale he had ever

told about the wonders of the forest or the pleasure of camping out on the plain could reassure
Bily. When Zluty spoke of how beautifully deep
and mysterious the forest was, Bily thought only
of how it would feel to be lost in the trackless,

lightless darkness beneath the dense canopy of leaves and branches. And what if Zluty never found his way out of the forest again? Or what if he did, but he came out the wrong side. What if, in his eagerness to get back into the light, Zluty rushed out and fell off the edge of the world?

However, Bily knew that they needed all that his brother brought back from the forest if they were to survive the long hard Winter, and so he tried not to talk of his fears.

Fortunately, aside from this one long journey, the other foraging trips Zluty made were shorter, the longest taking him away from the cottage for only two nights. There was a patch of deep flavourful orange roots that grew a day away from the cottage to the East. When these were in season Zluty would go and dig up enough to thicken stews and soups and to flavour bread for the whole Winter and drag them back to the cottage on a wheeled pallet he had made out of a piece of the egg that he and Bily had hatched from. Zluty always managed to return before dusk on the third day, despite stopping on the way to cut a load of sweetgrass to refresh their mattresses.

A day to the South of the cottage was a field

of the tough grass they used to weave roof tiles for the cottage. Zluty harvested the grass in mid-Autumn so that he and Bily would have enough time to weave the tiles and replace any that had become thin or ragged before Winter.

A half day South beyond the tough grass was a crop of wild rice. It grew in a patch of rare swampy ground on the bone-dry plain, and was inhabited by clouds of biting insects. To gather the rice, Zluty had to rub mud into his cheeks and hands to stop the insects biting him, and when entering the swamp he had to be very careful not to step on the blackclaw nests clustered all around the edges of the swamp. But the worst part was that he had to wade into black muddy water that reached right up to his middle.

A further half-day's walk was a field of wild wheat where Zluty harvested grain to grind into the flour Bily used to make bread and pancakes and pie crusts.

Not far from the wheat, to the East, was a wide field of sharp, unfriendly plants with prickles and fat bulbs that burst open at the end of Summer to reveal tight balls of white fluff. Zluty would gather the fluff balls into enormous light bales, and bring them back on his wheeled pallet for Bily to tease into fleece and spin into thread. During the long Winter he would weave the thread into cloth, or make it into felt for floor rugs.

Bily had tried to grow all of these wild crops in his garden so that Zluty would never have to travel away from the cottage save once a year when he went to the Northern Forest. But they did not prosper. Bily wondered if perhaps the foreign seeds that the birds had brought him had changed the earth about the cottage so that native plants and grasses would not grow there. Or maybe the wild seeds did not like to be captured and planted in a tamed patch of earth.

Whatever the reason, Bily had to accept that the trips Zluty made were needful. The truth was that

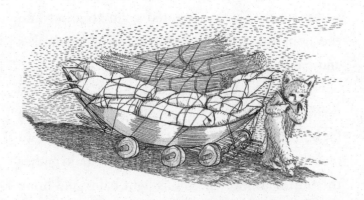

Zluty loved to tie his purple travelling scarf about his neck, shoulder his pack and set off across the plain. This might have saddened Bily, except that Zluty had once told him that he loved the cottage and its garden most of all when he was returning to it from a journey. He would first catch sight of it rising in a little hump from the flat plain, with a smudge of smoke above its chimney stack, and his heart would give a bound of joy. If it was dusk, he would see the light from the little lantern Bily always lit and stood it in the window after the sun set, facing the direction he had gone. Seeing it shining to welcome him, Zluty said his heart would ache with the gladness of coming home.

The life lived by the two brothers was very full and busy. As each season came and departed to give way to the next they always knew exactly what they had to do. This order and sameness was at the heart of Bily's contentment, and although Zluty loved to discover new things, and there were times when he dreamed of the deep and alluring mystery of the Northern Forest, he too was content with their lives. So day followed day and season followed season for many peaceful years and the two brothers went about their

tasks without either of them having any desire for change.

Yet change will come, whether it is wanted or not, and so it was that one morning on the day Zluty was to make his annual journey to the Northern Forest, change began to shape itself over their very heads.

2

Bily was at the stove carefully preparing the special complicated porridge he always made on this morning to fortify his brother and to keep himself busy so that he would not begin fretting before Zluty had even left the cottage. He was also finishing a pile of pancakes that were to be wrapped up in a woven cloth after they had cooled. They would serve as Zluty's supper that night when he stopped to camp on the plain.

Zluty was packing all of the things he would need for the journey, and thinking about a certain small dark-blue berry he had noticed the previous

year. It had been growing on a bush in one of the few shafts of sunlight that managed to penetrate the outer edge of the forest canopy. The birds that nested above had warned him that the berries were bad to eat, and so he had not bothered taking any. But a few nights earlier, Bily had been boiling feathergrass to concoct a new dye and sighing over the faintness of the blue colour it produced. Zluty, sanding the new walking staff he had made to take with him on his journey, had suddenly remembered the brightness of the blue berries and the richness of their colour and had made up his mind to bring some of them back as a surprise for Bily. He had already slipped an extra little pottery jar into his pack to hold the berries.

Zluty glanced above his bed at the beautiful hanging on the wall. Of all his possessions, he loved this best. The colours reminded him of the way the sunlight looked, filtering through the leaves in the Northern Forest. Bily had made it for his bed several years past and Zluty had loved it too much to allow it to be cut up for cleaning rags when Bily decided it was too thin and must be replaced. Zluty had insisted upon hanging it, and it looked so nice and unexpected on the wall that Bily had decided to make a special rug to hang above the long bench where they often sat and talked in the evenings when it was too warm for a fire.

The thought of his brother's delight at having a new colour to use made Zluty want to laugh aloud, but he reminded himself that he must first test the berries to make sure the dye was good before he gave them as a gift.

'I am going down to the digger mounds to see if they have milk,' Bily called from the door. 'Can you get the last pot of honey out of the cellar?'

'I will just as soon as I have finished this,' Zluty answered, grunting with the effort of tightening his pack. As he rolled the bedding so that he could bind it to the top of the pack it crackled loudly, for he had stuffed it with fresh sweetgrass the night before.

Bily came hurrying back inside and Zluty thought he must have forgotten the little wads of white fluff he traded to the diggers for milk, and which they used to soften their burrows. But his brother came straight over to him and said, 'Oh, Zluty, come and see. It's horrible!'

'Is it one of the birds?' Zluty asked. Many birds nested in the eaves of the cottage or in the bushes and small trees growing in the garden, and Bily appeared so upset that Zluty feared some harm must have come to Redwing, whom his brother dearly loved.

Bily caught hold of Zluty's hand. 'It is not any of the birds. It is the sky!' He tugged his brother through the cottage and out onto the step. 'Look!' Bily insisted, pointing away to the West.

Zluty's mouth fell open at the sight of a dark red stain spreading against the blue sky just above the horizon. It might have been a cloud saturated with the red dawn light, except it was in the West. He was alarmed, but a tiny part of him thrilled at the newness of it.

'What does it mean?' Bily asked. His frightened voice quenched the little spark of curiosity and excitement that had kindled in Zluty.

'It is only a storm cloud,' Zluty said in a reassuring voice.

'But a storm cloud is not red,' Bily objected.

He was right, Zluty thought, squinting his eyes

at the stain. He said at last, with more certainty than he felt, 'It is a mist. Mists are sometimes unusual colours, and it might simply have got that high by accident.'

Bily considered this, and then nodded slowly. 'A mist could get confused,' he said. 'It might have got too high and now it does not know how to get back down to the ground.'

'Exactly,' said Zluty, relieved to see that his brother's fluffed-up fur was beginning to settle. 'If you are nervous, I can easily put off the journey to the Northern Forest for a few days.'

Bily looked horrified. 'But you always go on the day after the first bellflower opens.'

Zluty saw then that in suggesting a change in their routine he had unsettled his brother even more than the queer sky, so he shook his head and pretended it had been a joke. 'Of course I am going to go today,' he said. 'As soon as I have had my porridge.'

Bily gave a sudden cry and thrust the wads of fluff he had been carrying into his brother's hand before running inside. Smiling, Zluty went down through the bushes and flowers and beyond the well to the flat dry ground where the diggers lived.

He carefully avoided the holes in the ground where there was a single nest of poisonous blackclaws and came to the hump of earth, which was the entrance to the network of burrows and tunnels where the community of diggers dwelt. He stamped his foot three times then squatted down to wait. His smile faded as he studied the red stain just above the Western horizon. It didn't really look much more like a mist than a storm cloud. But after all, what else could it be?

'Ra!' squeaked a voice, and Zluty turned his attention to the little digger that had emerged from the entrance to the hump. Zluty announced solemnly that he wished to trade for milk, and then he held out the wads that Bily had thrust into his hand. The digger twitched his shiny little black nose and crept forward to sniff suspiciously at the fluffs. At last he gave a soft 'Ra' and withdrew. Moments later, another two diggers appeared at the entrance. One of them carried a small mis-shapen mug of diggermilk.

The trade made, the diggers uttered polite squeaks of 'Ra!' before scurrying away with their prize. Getting to his feet carefully so as not to spill the milk, Zluty made his way back to the cottage. He regretted that he had not thought to point out the redness in the sky and ask the diggers what they made of it. Not that he would have learned much, for the little creatures had only a few words that meant many different things. Bily said the meaning was all in how those few words were said, but he spent more time with the diggers than Zluty because they liked to come and watch him when he was at the clay pit by the well, making pots.

'I wish I knew how they make them,' Bily said, skimming off the cream and then transferring the milk from the digger mugs into the jug they would put on the table. He held up one of the digger mugs and studied it closely. 'The shape is bad, but light goes through the stuff they are made of, and I am thinking how nice it would be if I could make a cover for the windows from it so that we need not have the shutters closed in Winter. It would let in some light and we would not need to use so many candles. Imagine how pretty it would be with the sun shining through it.'

Zluty carried the jug of milk to the table, which was already set for his breakfast. He could tell from Bily's chatter about the digger mugs that his brother did not want to talk about the queer sky, and so he merely held out his bowl for the hot porridge to be served and then poured on some of the warm creamy diggermilk and dribbled in a little honey and a sprinkling of nuts and dried berries.

Bily served his own porridge and then there was no talk for a time.

Zluty was still eating the porridge when Bily left the table to wrap up the pancakes and pack them into the space Zluty had left for them.

'You have not packed neatly enough, for there is less space than usual,' he grumbled.

Zluty finished the last mouthful of porridge and hurried over to take the pancakes from his brother before Bily emptied the pack and dis-covered the extra jar he had put in to hold the berries. 'You see, there is plenty of room for them, and they won't be the least bit squashed,' he insisted as he carefully put the pancakes inside one of the bigger pots. He fastened the top flap of the pack and tied his travelling scarf jauntily about his neck.

Bily helped him put on his pack, and then Zluty took up his new staff and went outside to get his water bottles. These were small and there were many of them. He must carry enough water to travel the full four days to the Northern For-est, and it was easier to carry it in small amounts hung evenly all about him. There were only two springs on the plain. One was beside the cottage and the other was inside a rift in the ground near the Northern Forest. Bily helped him attach the last of the bottles to hooks on the woven strap that ran across Zluty's chest, and then the two brothers hugged one another warmly.

'Travel safe and return soon,' Bily said, trying to be brave and cheerful.

'I will, I promise,' Zluty replied, resisting the desire to reassure his brother about the odd sky, for that would only make him worry all the more. But he was glad to see Redwing glide down to sit in the bush nearest the door, where his brother lifted his hand in farewell. The black-and-red bird gave a trill of farewell and Zluty bowed to her to thank her for her good wishes – he supposed that was what she was saying – and then he set off, his heart lifting at the sight of the distant forest, despite the strangeness of the sky.

3

ily stood watching Zluty until he was no
more than a yellow dab of brightness on
the stony plain. Redwing made a little
sympathetic noise in her throat.

'I wish he did not have to go,' Bily confessed
softly to himself, and although he had not meant
to look, his eyes flickered away to the West and
the strange, horrible redness in the sky. It was not
the pretty scarlet of Redwing's tip feathers, but a
dark heavy red that reminded him unpleasantly
of blood. The thought of the sky bleeding made
his stomach hurt but he told himself that it was

only hunger he was feeling. He ought to go in and finish his breakfast. He had eaten a few mouthfuls to keep Zluty company but his mind had been on the pancakes and his brother's looming journey.

Leaving the door ajar so that Redwing could come in if she liked, Bily went back into the cottage. He was immediately reassured by the sight of all the familiar things around him. If he tried hard, he could make himself believe that Zluty had only gone for the day and that he would be back when the sun set. Sometimes when Zluty was away and Bily felt lonely, he did that, but he never felt he could do it when Zluty went to the Northern Forest. It was too great and solemn a journey, and since Zluty must endure the danger and hardship of it, Bily felt he ought at least to endure his loneliness.

He ate his porridge, enjoying the taste of the honey that flavoured it. He would use the remainder of it to make a rich honey cake. He would then hide it away in the cellar and bring it out to serve for their mid-Winter supper. Thinking of the Winter to come turned Bily's thoughts to the dyes, for that was when he did most of his weaving. He especially wanted a deep clear blue, and the thin colour he had got from his last experiment was no use to him. But perhaps he could turn it into a delicate shade of purple by adding a little of another colour dye. It would not go to waste for he needed purple as well as blue for the special wall hanging he would make. The difficulty in making dyes was that the colour that came from the thing he boiled was often quite different to the colour of the thing. For instance, his best yellow dye came from a vivid pink petal. And two dyes mixed together did not always produce the colour he expected. To achieve a certain colour meant days of experimenting.

Bily pushed the interesting and complicated question of dyes to the back of his mind and set about putting the cottage in order. He washed the dishes and dried them, and wiped down the table and stove, then he set the pancakes he had made for his own supper in the cool cupboard and scrubbed and oiled the table. Finally, he swept the

floor and remade Zluty's bed, which his brother never made quite smooth enough to satisfy Bily.

This done, he had a drink of hot honey cordial and made up his mind that instead of going outside to garden straightaway, as he usually did, he would occupy himself with some spinning. But when he went down into the cellar to fetch his bag of white fluffs, he noticed that several of the older pottery urns had begun to crack. He ought to do some potting while Zluty was away. Aside from some new urns, he could make a new mug to replace the one Zluty had dropped the week before. But digging up clay and making pottery were outside jobs and he did not want to go outside until the sky was its proper self. He got a basket full of white fluffs and his spindle and carried them upstairs, thinking that he would have plenty of time to make pots before Zluty came back. Then he settled himself contentedly by the fire and began to spin the fluffs into thread. Redwing, who liked the movement of the spindle, soon came in to keep him company, and for a time Bily was far too absorbed to think about his brother or the sky.

That afternoon, Zluty came upon a vast new patch of sweetgrass. The wind must have blown some of the seeds here from the field closer to the cottage, which he had passed that morning. It was odd that the seeds did not mind being carried here by the wind, but had refused to grow when he had carried them back to the cottage. Perhaps

Bily was right and there were some seeds that needed to be wild.

The thought of his brother made Zluty feel uneasy, because he knew Bily would be fretting over him and over the red stain in the Western sky. He was sure that the strange mist would vanish by nightfall, but until then, Bily would fret.

Zluty wished he had suggested that Bily come with him to the Northern Forest, but even if his home-loving brother had agreed to such a dramatic change in routine, it would have made things very hard for them in the seasons to come. Zluty knew that his foraging was important for their survival, but so were all of the things Bily did at the cottage. It took both of them to collect and prepare all they needed. Zluty could still remember the terrible Winters they had endured after one of the wild crops they relied upon had failed during the year, and another time when he had fallen ill and had been unable to do his share.

That had not happened for a long time because they had a lot more than they needed stored in the cave cellar now, in case of an emergency, but the memory of the hungry Winters was very strong.

To distract himself from his concern about Bily,

and from his weariness, for he had not stopped at midday to rest and eat as he usually did, Zluty took out his little green pipe and began to play a soft tune as he walked. The song wove the steady tread of his feet into the rushy whispering of the sweet-grass and for a time he tramped along contentedly, lost in the sweet scent of the grass and the sweetness of making a song. But even with the song to distract him, once dusk came, he could not make himself go on any further. He was so tired that he did not trouble to light a fire when he stopped. He merely moved the biggest stones from a little patch of ground where he would lay out his bedroll, ate some dried fruit and nuts, and stretched out to sleep.

The next morning, when Zluty awoke, he was dismayed to find the sun was already high above the horizon. He had slept in, wasting the time he had made up the day before by skipping his midday meal.

He rolled his bed hastily, tied it to his pack and set off at once. He wanted to try to reach the Northern Forest a half-day earlier than usual so that he would have time to gather the blue berries for Bily's dye without lengthening his trip. If he could travel fast enough, he might even have time to venture a little deeper into the forest than usual.

In the past, it had been impossible to think of it. The farthest he had ever gone was to the great circular mounded bank of earth where he collected mushrooms. It had been simply too dark to go any deeper into the forest. As it was, he had had to sniff his way to the mushrooms and collect them by feel. Looking back from the earthbank, he could just see the faint greenish light that was the edge of the forest.

Once, Zluty had tried bringing a candle into the forest so that he could go beyond the mushrooms. He had planned to leave a trail of pebbles that would guide him back out, but he had barely taken ten steps into the trees before the flame flickered out.

A lantern proved no better. There was something thick and heavy in the air under the trees that stifled flame. Zluty had always longed to go deeper into the forest, but without a trustworthy source of light he had dared not risk it.

He had pushed all thoughts of exploration to the back of his mind until one morning near Summer

when he had gone to collect the white fluff balls
that Bily spun into thread. He had almost filled his
collection bags when he noticed one of the small
hard boulders that sometimes fell burning from

the sky at night. It had hit a rocky hump of earth and cracked open. Spilling out of its hollow middle was a glittering flow of stones as clear and gleaming as the ice that formed on the well during Winter.

Zluty had collected the stones with delight. He decided to give Bily the prettiest one, and the largest would serve as a better cutter for the tough sweetgrass than his stone knife, if he could find a way to mount it in a handle.

But that night, back at the cottage, when he had brought the stones to show Bily, they had both gasped as a pale cloud of light flowed out of the cloth pouch. The stones gave off their own light, and the darker it became, the brighter they shone. Zluty had thought at once of using the shining stones to lay a trail deeper into the Northern Forest, though of course he had said nothing of this to Bily.

Zluty had been eager to try the stones on this trip, but looking at the sky when he woke, he was startled to find that the red mist had not gone away in the night. He was not really anxious about the mist, but he had seen how Bily had pretended he was not afraid when they had parted and did not want to give his brother cause for more worry. He was determined not to lengthen his trip. The only way he could explore or spend time searching for the blue berries was if he could make up enough time to do it. No matter what, he must be home within ten days.

Glancing back over his shoulder at the red mist, Zluty realised it had grown and wondered if a wind was pushing it Northward. Somehow it did not surprise him that the mist had come from the West. That was a way he never went, for the plain was at its most barren in that direction.

4

Bily woke the next morning to the sweet scent of the honey cake he had baked the previous day. He was especially pleased because he had managed to stretch out the honey to make a batch of small honey nut cakes, which he meant to serve as part of the welcome home feast he was planning for Zluty. His brother loved honey cake better than anything – the crunchiness of the nuts mixed up with the sweetness of the honey. Bily sat up and stretched deliciously, but when he opened his eyes his spirits fell. The window above his bed looked to the West, and the awful red mist that had come up the morning Zluty left the cottage now covered so much of the sky that the plain below was bathed in its dreadful bloody colour.

Bily got out of bed and padded across to look out the window on the other side of the cottage. From this direction, the early morning sun was shining down on the garden out of a pure blue sky. There was not a hint of red in the light, and Bily gazed out for a long time before he went to wash his face and hands and brush his fur.

This was the third day of Zluty's journey. Tomorrow evening, he would arrive at the Forest. He would sleep the night, and the following day – the fifth day – he would tap the trees and collect mushrooms. The sixth day he would collect the tree sap and get the honey from the forest bees and that night he would cook some pancakes and refill all of his water bulbs. Early on the seventh day he would be ready to set off for the cottage.

How Bily wished it were already the tenth day and that Zluty was arriving home. Then he chided himself, for if it were the tenth day the new mug he had made for Zluty yesterday would not be ready. He had also made an urn for honey, and a particularly nice bowl. Tomorrow the clay would

be dry enough for him to fire them in his little kiln.
Then he had only to glaze the pots and fire them
a last time.

Thinking about glazes, he carried the heavy
honey cakes down to the cellar and then he carried

up a basket of ground cones to feed to the fire. He was just spreading some toast with the digger butter when Redwing swooped through the window and came to land on the arm of his chair. He fed her some crumbs and tried to feel content, but he could not help but picture Zluty, waking in his bedroll on the bare plain with the unnatural red sky arching above him. He did not know how Zluty could bear it, even knowing how brave he was.

'I wish he would never have to go to the Northern Forest again,' Bily said fiercely.

An odd silence fell and Bily suddenly felt frightened, for the words he had uttered were no less than a wish for change. He tugged his mind away from the red mist and from thoughts of Zluty, and set himself to scour the cottage from top to bottom. He washed and polished all of the pots, trimmed the candles and renewed the paper on the lanterns. When the fire had gone out, he raked out the embers and swept the hearthstones before laying another fire ready to be lit. He tidied all of the cupboards and shelves in the cottage and pulled the rugs together in a pile by the door, to be beaten outside. He swept and mopped the floor and then steeled himself to go outside.

'You went out yesterday,' he pointed out sternly to himself.

But that had only been briefly to fetch water and clay which he had brought inside to mould, even though he usually did his potting outside. *And the red mist was smaller yesterday*, said a frightened voice in his mind.

'Just because I am frightened doesn't mean I have to let that stop me from doing what I need to do,' he told Redwing, and with that, he took a deep breath to steady himself, and opened the door. Steadfastly keeping his back to the West, he brought the rugs out onto the step. One by one he draped them over a bush and beat them thoroughly before carrying them back inside.

When he had finished the rugs, Bily went to draw a bucket of water from the well. He had noticed the delicate bellflowers growing nearby were drooping unhappily and he was ashamed that he had let his fear of the sky stop him from bringing them water the previous day. To make up for it, he gave every plant and bush and tree in the garden a good long drink and then he got himself a mug of water from the well.

As he drank, he forced himself to look at the sky.

Could that terrible redness really be a mist? he wondered. Yet if it was not a mist, then what could it be, spreading slowly and monstrously eastward?

Redwing flew down and alighted on the rim

of the well, tilting her head to fix him with one bright eye. She gave a soft trill and he sighed and gathered her into his arms, stroking her crest feathers. 'I know the sky can't hurt me, Redwing, but it makes me feel strange to see it looking so wrong. It would be the same as if Zluty came back from the Northern Forest turned green or with a third ear on top of his head.'

Redwing gave a little chirrup as he set her down again and Bily shrugged. 'I *know* it would still be Zluty, but it would mean something about him had changed.'

Redwing fluffed her wings.

'I just don't like things changing, that's all,' Bily muttered.

He went to the cellar to fetch his dye-making box and carried it out to the bench under the largest bush in the garden. He was determined to see if he could make the too-pale blue dye into a more interesting colour. He had some paper and he made notes and marks as he tried this and that combination, so that he would remember how to make the dye if he chanced upon a good colour. This reminded him that he ought to make some more sheets of paper for this was the last piece and

Zluty liked to map anything new that he had found on his journey to the forest.

A slight breeze had begun to blow, flipping the edge of the paper and making the leaves rustle, but Bily was concentrating too hard even to notice it.

Far across the plain to the North, Zluty felt the same breeze and gave a shiver of delight, for walking was hot work when the sun was shining down so brightly and he was pushing himself harder than usual to make up for sleeping in the day before. He had not been thinking of the red sky, but when he turned his face to the wind, which was coming from the West, he saw how it was spreading in the sky behind him and his mood darkened. It was clear to him now that it was not growing but moving Northward even as he was.

That meant it was also getting closer to the cottage.

Zluty was troubled but it was too late to turn back. He had walked into the night and was a good deal closer to the green shadow on the horizon that was the Northern Forest than he would usually have been on the third day. Besides, red mist or not, they needed the tree sap and honey

and mushrooms to last through the harsh cold dry
Winter on the plain. The best thing was to do what
he had come to do and get home as fast as possible.

He had already decided when he woke and saw that the mist had not gone, that there would be no exploration or berry hunt this time. His sole aim now was to get home as soon as possible.

He put down his pack and unhooked one of the water bulbs to drink. Moving more quickly meant he was drinking more than he usually did and this was his last bulb. He was careful as he stoppered it, for Bily had made the bulbs thin so they would weigh less and they were now very fragile. One year Zluty had tripped and, in a single disastrous moment, had broken four bulbs, losing all the precious water they held. It had been exactly halfway through the second day of his journey home and he had been fevered from thirst by the time he staggered into the cottage.

And yet, despite the dangers of the journey and his dislike of worrying Bily, despite even the red mist, Zluty loved this march across the plain. Bily said it must be terribly dull to walk for days on end across the flat emptiness, but it was not dull at all. You soon saw that the plain was not truly empty either. Aside from diggers, there were many different sorts of insects and small plants, and even when there were no plants, there were pools of colour in the slight dips and rises of the land which changed constantly as the day rearranged shadows and light.

Zluty had never been able to explain to Bily why crossing the barren plain filled him with such joy, because he was not sure himself. But it had something to do with being alone in all that strong hot brightness, carrying all that he needed on his own back.

Bily lamented over how tired Zluty must be at the end of each long and lonely day of walking, and how horrid it must be to lie down on the hard ground with the vast open vault of the sky curving overhead. But if Zluty was weary, it was a good kind of weariness that made his blood sing and his heart lie quiet within his chest. Impossible to explain that he even liked the heaviness of the pack dragging at his shoulders. As for sleeping on the hard ground with the stars and the open sky above, Zluty thought that might just be the thing he loved best of all.

But there were not words enough to make Bily understand. It might be possible to play a tune that captured some of what he felt about the journey across the plain, but in the end, the only way his brother could ever truly understand would be to try it for himself. There were some things that could not be told or shown, but must be felt.

That whole afternoon, Zluty tramped steadily over the most barren stretch of the journey. There were no insects and no plants and it was hot despite the constant breeze flowing from the West like one endless cool breath. The only things that moved were his shadow lengthening as the sun

made its own slow journey overhead, and the green forest growing larger and more distinct the nearer he came to it. Then, in the afternoon, the sun was swallowed up by the bleary redness spreading out across the Western sky, and hours before dusk Zluty found himself walking through a murky brown twilight.

But Zluty did not stop until it began to get dark, and when he set down his pack his weariness seemed to fall into him like a great weight. The wind was gritty with sand and so he lay out his bedroll in the lee of one of the metal objects that littered the plain. The longing to lie down and sleep was nearly irresistible.

He had to force himself to gather a few ground cones and scoop out a little fire-pit. Then he sat down on his bed and dug out his flints and some white fluffs. When the cones were crackling brightly, he rummaged in his pack for a pot and made a simple stew from some water and a few bits of dried root and mushroom. As he waited for it to cook, he unwrapped a scone Bily had made and bit into it. It was dry now but very good and he felt less light-headed after eating it. He was suddenly glad he had made a proper meal. The previous night he had simply eaten some nuts before sleeping.

He tipped the stew into a bowl and ate it hungrily. It tasted especially delicious, as all food seemed to when eaten out on the plain. Perhaps it was because the food carried the memory of home, which never seemed sweeter to Zluty than when he was away from it.

When he had finished eating, Zluty scoured the pot and mug and spoon with sand and packed everything away into his pack. By his reckoning, he had made up enough time to arrive at the forest by midday tomorrow, rather than late in the evening. That meant he would be able to tap the trees for sap straightaway rather than having to wait until the next morning.

It took a whole night and day for the thick dark sap to fill the pots, and being able to begin when he arrived meant the pots would be full by nightfall. During the day he would gather the mushrooms and get the honey and he ought to be able to set off for home on the morning of the sixth day, rather than on the seventh. That would bring him back to the cottage a whole day earlier. Zluty did not want to lose any of his hard-won extra time by waking late again so he lay down and closed his eyes.

He was so tired that he had thought he would fall asleep at once, but as sometimes happens, his weariness was so great that sleep would not come.

He found himself picturing Bily fighting a grass fire alone. It was something that had happened once when he had been away from the cottage, and Bily had managed well enough. But the fire had happened when Zluty had been less than a day away from the cottage, and it had been Summer, when they always dug a wide firebreak in the prickly wiregrass that surrounded the cottage, and kept buckets of earth and water in a line along the back wall of the cottage.

'It is not Summer,' Zluty reminded himself, sitting up and putting his last two ground cones on the embers, for the breeze had made the night cool. Sparks coiled up into the dark dry air as they caught light, and Zluty lay down again to watch them. Finally, he slept and dreamed of a creature red as blood, red as the heartstones of a fire, running across the ground, setting alight everything it touched.

5

Bily felt that something was wrong even before he was properly awake, and when he opened his eyes and found himself bathed in reddish light, he shuddered. Sitting up, he saw that the red mist now covered the sky. He climbed out of his bed and hurried to the East-facing window. As he had feared, the redness reached far enough around that he could see it from this window, too. And it was no longer simply a colour, for it was now close enough for him to see that it moved and roiled like the thick heavy smoke that came from a fire made of green ground cones.

The plants and bushes in the garden stirred and shifted restlessly as if they disliked the unnatural red light as much as he did.

Bily went into the kitchen and made himself

porridge for breakfast. He was halfway through eating it when he suddenly realised that he had not heard the birds singing when he awakened. Usually the morning rang with their calls and songs. He told himself that the unnatural sky had put the birds out of their routine, but his heart was beating swiftly as he went to the front door and opened it.

The door faced North, which was the way Zluty had gone, and here at least, the sky was reassuringly blue. Bily went out into the garden and made his way through the vegetable patch to the fruit trees. He was relieved to see that there *were* a few birds here and there, clinging to swaying branches, though not nearly as many as there ought to have been, and all were unnaturally silent. Bily went to the tree that grew by the outside cellar trapdoor, which was home to a family of small brown birds that spent their days squabbling and threatening one another. Its branches were empty. He went around to the back of the cottage where ground cones were piled up to dry out in the sun before being shifted into the cellar. Above the pile, under the eaves, were nests of clay fixed to the rock wall, but when he looked into them, he found only three birds. The rest were empty.

Bily did not know what to make of it. He whistled to Redwing and was relieved when she uttered her soft, high call. He found her sitting on one of the hard metal objects that littered the plain. This one was barely visible under the coils of a night-flowering creeper. In the reddish light of the sky, Redwing's feathers glowed beautifully crimson as she fluffed up her plumage and chirped a greeting.

Bily was so relieved to see her behaving normally that he put his arms around her and pressed his cheek gently to her head before asking if she knew what had made so many of the birds fly away before they would usually leave for the Winter.

Redwing gave an expressive trill, but Bily could not quiet his thoughts and fears enough to make out what she was saying. It was something to do with the birds being frightened. She gave another earnest trill and he made himself concentrate. She was telling him the only birds that remained other than her were those with eggs yet to hatch or nestlings too young to fly. The parent birds were not singing because they feared what would happen to them and their young.

'Are they afraid of the red mist?' Bily asked.

Redwing chirped that they were afraid the red wind would kill their eggs and nestlings.

Bily thought he must have misunderstood her, for Zluty had said the redness was a mist. He would have asked further questions of Redwing, except that he noticed one of the long strands of a creeper that usually attached itself to the side of the cottage was flying free. If left untended the whole bank of it might be torn away by the buffeting wind.

Bily ran inside to get twine and his stone knife, and set about binding the creeper up. As he worked, he realised that his fur was beginning to fluff. That and the growing strength of the wind were sure signs that a storm was brewing. He ought to be relieved that the mysterious redness might only be a storm after all. Except the birds had never flown away because of a storm before.

Bily tied up the creeper, then he tied up all of the vines and staked the tomato plants and the bellflowers, just in case. As he worked, he made up his mind that when he was finished he would try to convince the birds to let him carry their nests into the cellar. He could open the outer trapdoor, and they could fly in and out as they pleased.

Zluty woke at dawn, and set off at once with only a handful of nuts for his breakfast. By midmorning he could see the Northern Forest clearly, though it would still take him several hours to reach it. The wind blowing from the West was much stronger than it had been the day before, and the redness had unfurled like a great cloak across the sky to the South and the East. The wind did not hamper him as it would have done if he had been walking into it, but its constant side shoves were wearisome. The sooner he reached the forest the better, for not only would he be able to get out of the wind but he would also be able to drink. He had run out of water that morning and the wind was making him terribly thirsty. Even so, he decided he would not stop until he reached the spring cave.

Just on midday, when the sun was directly overhead, Zluty was startled to find himself in the midst of a buzzing cloud of bees.

He stopped, startled to see bees so far from the forest. Then he realised they would not have flown so far – they must have a ground hive nearby. Despite his thirst and his impatience to reach the forest, Zluty pricked his ears at the thought.

Honey from the plains had a special flavour that he and Bily liked very much. If the bees would give him some, he could put it into the extra pot he had brought, and give that to Bily as a gift instead of the blue berries.

Before he could ask, the bees began to hum. He

listened carefully to their beesong and was astonished to be told that his coming had been foreseen
by their Queen who wished to speak with him.
She could not fly, being wingless, so he must come
to the hive. It was not far, they promised.

'What need have you?' Zluty asked courteously,
lying on his belly and stretching out his hand so
that the great lustrous Queen bee could clamber
onto it. Then he sat up, holding her very carefully
as her subjects hovered anxiously, and tilted his ear
to hear her song.

'I dreamed that you made the earth about the hive flat so that it was safe from the great earth bird. When you refused, the terrible earth bird whose purpose was to destroy all life gouged up the hive. My subjects tried to build up the earth but they were too slow. I and all of the fledgling queens were killed. The hive was doomed, for a hive must have a Queen.'

Zluty had no idea what an earth bird could be, but only a bird full of madness would attack a hive and risk being stung to death. Most likely he had misunderstood, for bees always spoke as if everything had already happened, even when they were talking about the future. He might have asked more questions if he had time to sit and listen over and over to their songs, but instead he merely agreed to do as the Queen asked.

He took from his pack the small wooden spade he used to shovel earth over the embers of his campfires, and set about laying a good cover of earth around the hump that was the upper part of the hive. By the time he had finished, there was no longer a dip with a hump in the middle of it, but flat ground. If he had glanced in this direction now, Zluty would not even have noticed the hive.

The bees busied themselves tidying the new entrance, and when Zluty bent to lift the Queen down to it from the pack where she had waited as he worked, she told him he had taken some honeycomb and a bee with him, and that she had dreamed of a hive that had been set up in the vale of bellflowers at the end of his journeying.

Zluty was puzzled. The Queen seemed to be offering him a fledgling bee queen, for a hive could only be set up by a new queen, but what did she mean about the vale of bellflowers? Perhaps she meant the cottage. No doubt the little bed of bell-flowers Bily nurtured by the well would seem like a vale to a tiny bee queen whose hive was situated on such stony ground, and certainly the cottage was the end of his journey.

It surprised him that the Queen of the plain hive knew what a bellflower was. Perhaps she had seen one on her maiden flight before she lost her wings. Occasionally, flowers did bloom on the plain after rare rainfall. Though it must have rained very hard to bring bellflowers to life, for they needed a lot of watering.

'You want me to take a queen bee?' Zluty asked, to be sure he had not misunderstood.

'You took a small queen and three males,' the Queen agreed, even as a cluster of bees emerged from the newly tidied entrance to the hive carrying a small chunk of honeycomb upon which sat a very small bee.

Zluty got out the little pottery jar he had intended for the blue berries, trying to imagine Bily's delight at having a hive in his own garden. Once it was established, Zluty would never need to bring honey from the forest again. That meant he could carry more tree sap or mushrooms.

The bees flew busily back and forth bringing more and more honeycomb to the jar until the Queen pronounced it was enough to last the bees to the end of their journey. It was far more honey than a few bees would eat in five or six days, Zluty thought, but he said nothing for it would be poor thanks to the Queen for such a magnificent gift if he showed his impatience to be gone.

He put the jar carefully into the top of his pack, leaving the stopper out so that his bees could breathe, then he rubbed his hands with sand until they were no longer sticky, and came to thank the Queen. She had gone back inside the hive, but the bees sang her gratitude for saving the hive from the earth bird before they all swarmed into the hive after her.

Finally, three male bees remained and they sang that they had accompanied him on his great journey to the vale of the bellflowers. Zluty bid them fly into the top of the jar carrying the little queen and then carefully hoisted his pack onto his shoulders.

Zluty set off quickly for he had lost several hours in coming to the hive and he needed to get to the Northern Forest early enough to set the tree taps before night fell.

He glanced back at the redness growing in the sky. The wind had grown stronger. He wondered if, after all, the redness was a storm cloud. He would know soon enough, for it was drawing closer behind him and would eventually reach the ground hive.

It might very well be what the Queen had meant when she had sung about the earth bird that would endanger the hive, Zluty thought. Certainly the spreading redness did look like the wings of a vast bird. Though what a storm had to do with the earth, he could not guess.

Zluty puzzled for a time over what the bee Queen had said about the earth bird wanting to destroy all life, before deciding that he had probably misunderstood – for how could a storm be said to want anything?

It was late in the afternoon before Zluty reached the narrow rift where the spring cave lay. Beyond it, the vast Northern Forest rose up like a cool dense dream.

Zluty went down into the cave, set his pack down carefully and threw himself on his belly to slake his thirst at the cold pool of water that lay at the base of the spring. Then he lay out his bedroll, resisting the impulse to lie down for a little and rest. He had to get the tree taps in place before the sun set.

He unfastened his collection bag from the front of the pack and, being careful not to wake the sleeping bees, he took out the bee jar and set it aside. Then he dug out the tree sap pots, the tap tubes he had whittled, and the hammer he would use to drive them into the tree trunks. Putting everything into his collection bag, he slung it over his shoulder and took up his staff.

Coming out of the rift, Zluty was startled at the force of the wind, which seemed to have redoubled in the little time he had been in the cave. The redness now filled half the sky and he was suddenly certain that it was a storm and, given the wind, it would surely reach the forest not long after dusk.

Then, with a stab of disquiet, he realised that it must already have reached the cottage and Bily.

6

Bily had just finished carrying the last of the nests down into the cellar. It had taken him over an hour to persuade each bird that if the wind became any stronger it was likely to dislodge his or her nest. He had no doubt now that there was a storm coming, whether or not it was the redness in the sky or merely the thing pushing it. Aside from the growing force of the wind, his fur was fully fluffed. The birds knew it, too, yet without Redwing, Bily doubted he would have managed to convince them to let him shift their nests. Most of the parent birds had come down to the cellar with their nests, but there were a few who were too frightened. They were desperate to be reunited with their babies but they needed help to overcome their fear. Bily was crumbling some bread into a bowl to set in the cellar beneath the open trapdoor as an encouragement for them, when he heard a tearing noise from above.

He thought at once of the roof tiles.

Since midday the rising wind had been plucking and worrying at them. Though well made and carefully tied down, the woven tiles had yet to be repaired and strengthened for the Winter to come. If the wind managed to tear away one of the tiles, it was possible that, bit by bit, the rest would be torn away, and even if only a few patches in the roof were opened up, rain would get inside the cottage once the storm struck. It seldom rained on the plain, but Bily could smell it on the wind.

Opening the front door to go out and look at the roof, Bily was startled at how much stronger the wind had become. All of the bushes and plants were bent over under its force and some had even been completely stripped of their leaves. No wonder most of the birds had flown away.

He backed away from the cottage to see the roof better.

It was dark because of the dull red sky, but he saw at once that the wind had torn away almost a whole line of tiles along the western side of the roof. Bily knew he ought to get the ladder and climb up onto the roof to tie the remaining tiles down, but the wind was so strong that he dared not try it. If only Zluty had been there to do it – he had no fear of heights.

Bily wrung his hands for a moment, wishing hopelessly for his brother, but he knew that Zluty could not help him now. This knowledge frightened him, but it steadied him, too, and let him see there was only one thing he could do.

Casting a final glance at the boiling red clouds drawing nearer every second, he ran back inside the house, wrenched open the cellar doors and began to roll up the rugs and push them down the steps. He took down the rug that hung over Zluty's bed, and bundled up the bedding from both of their beds, pushing it all down into the cellar. Next, he carried down his weaving, the spindle and the bowl of breadcrumbs. Lighting a lantern he kept at the bottom of the steps, he was pleased to see that most of the birds were now sitting on the nests that he had tucked here and there.

He pushed the rugs and bedding to one side of the cellar, and went back up into the cottage to bring down his collection of feathers.

Puffing slightly as he made yet another trip down the steps, Bily prayed that all of his work

would be for nothing, and that the roof tiles would hold. But even as he came up again from the cellar, he heard a long ominous ripping sound.

At the same moment he realised that he had forgotten to bring in any water. He did not want to face the tempest outside again, but there was nothing for it. He got two big urns and opened the door. The wind snatched it from his hands and threw it open with a loud bang before pushing at Bily as if it meant to knock him down.

Bily braced himself and shouldered his way outside, hauling out the urns after him and then dragging the door closed behind him. The garden heaved and churned in the heavy red light that suffused the late afternoon, making it seem to have come alive.

Bily dragged the urns around to the well and

drew up buckets of water until he had filled them. Then he rolled them one at a time to the outside entrance to the cellar. Flinching from branches that lashed and flailed at him, he lowered first one urn and then the other into the cellar cave using a hook on a rope that ran up through another hook attached to outside of the cottage.

Propping the cellar door open so that the birds would not feel trapped, Bily ran back around the house to the door, noticing as he did so that two lines of the woven roof tiles had been torn off and the ones at the end of another line had begun to flap. There was nothing he could do, of course, but his heart ached as he went inside and saw the dark red sky was showing through the tiles in three separate places.

One of the shutters he had closed earlier rattled free of its hook, and the clatter it made as it banged open made his heart leap against his chest. He gathered his wits and ran to catch hold of it and push it closed. Even as he lifted the hook back into place, there was a great rushing roar outside that shook the cottage, and then came a cacophonous clattering and thudding on the roof and walls as if a hundred Zluty's were outside hurling stones at the cottage.

Having no idea what was happening, Bily froze and waited for the terrible noise to stop. But it went on and on. He forced himself to go to the other side of the cottage where the tiles had been torn away so that he could look out. To his astonishment, he saw that great red stones were falling out of the sky. Even as he watched, several crashed through the hole to land on the rug below.

For a time he stood gaping at them in disbelief, then the large beams of wood overhead creaked ominously. Bily thought with horror of the red stones piling up on top of the roof, growing heavier and heavier, and backed away from the torn opening. He had been worried that things would get wet or be ruined, but now he saw there was a far greater danger.

Calling to Redwing, who was perched on the back of his chair by the fire, he ran to the cellar doors. Before he could descend the steps, he heard a violent crash from below. A moment later the birds that had taken refuge in the cellar exploded up into the cottage in a wild flurry of feathers and beaks, screeching, 'Monster! Monster!'

'Come back!' cried Bily in alarm, as the birds looped and swooped in the air, knowing they

would be killed if the roof of the cottage gave way
under the stones. He was sure that their monster
was only the door to the outside cellar entrance
blowing shut in the wind. If only he had closed the

outside trapdoor to the cellar after he had lowered the water urns!

'There is no monster,' Bily shouted, trying desperately to make himself heard over the screeching of the birds and the thunderous noise of the falling stones. 'It is only the storm. We must go back down into the cellar where it is safe.'

None of the birds would listen and Bily saw that he would have to go down into the cellar to show them there was nothing to fear. When he was not devoured, the birds would realise they had made a mistake and return to their nests. On impulse, he took up the broom standing against the wall near the cellar opening before beginning to climb down the steps. The light given out by the lantern he had left on the bottom step was weak and fitful and Bily realised there must be very little oil left in its reservoir. He nearly groaned aloud but reminded himself that at least the jug of oil was in the cellar.

As he descended, the weight of earth between him and the cottage muffled the sound of the falling stones until Bily could only hear the soft swift thudding of his own heart. He realised that he was frightened and told himself sternly that

there was no monster waiting to eat him in the
cellar. Just the same, he was glad he had taken
the broom.

By the time he got to the bottom step, Bily's
mouth was dry with fear. He knew that there
was no such thing as a monster. But the thought
came to him that if someone had told him the
day before that stones would rain from the sky,

he would have said that there was no such thing as a stone storm.

Bily peered around the cellar. He could just make out the humped shapes of bales of sweet-grass, sacks of grain and ground flour and the bedding he had thrown down earlier. Turning slowly, he ran his eyes along the rows of empty honey and tree sap jugs. Everything was exactly as it ought to be, except that when he looked down to the lower end of the sloping cellar, he saw that the trapdoor to the other entrance was completely smashed, splintered bits of it hanging down around the opening. Some stones had fallen through the gap, knocking over the ladder that usually rested against the wall under the trapdoor, but fortunately the water urns had not been broken.

Bily set down the broom and ran to roll the urns out of danger, thinking that the bush growing by the entrance must be partly shielding the open-ing for only a few stones had fallen into the cellar. None were big enough to have stove the door in and he wondered if the tree had been uprooted by the wind and had fallen on it.

One of the baby birds began to cheep piteously behind him, reminding Bily of the danger faced by the birds up in the cottage. He ran back up the steps and, to his relief, he found that most of the birds were now perched around the cellar doors peering down fearfully at him. Above them, Bily saw that there were now several places where the weight of the stones had torn holes in the roof. Worse, right above the cellar door, the roof tiles were sagging heavily.

'Come into the cellar before the stones come through the roof!' he begged the birds. 'There is no monster and your eggs and nestlings grow cold.'

He looked at Redwing, who immediately launched herself through the opening. To his relief, the rest of the birds followed her. As soon as they had all come into the cellar, Bily reached up to close the doors over his head.

It was not a moment too soon, for he heard a loud ripping noise and a great clamour of stones falling. He went back down the steps again, careful not to stand on any of the birds. Clearly, they were not going to go any further into the cellar without him, even though Redwing had flown down to where the lantern stood. Its flame was almost out when he reached the bottom of the steps and Bily carried it over to the shelf by the

bales of sweetgrass, where he kept the lantern oil.
But even as he set it down he froze, for there, in
the corner of the cellar, was a pair of huge glowing
yellow eyes.

7

Entering the vast and mysterious Northern Forest, Zluty was struck as always by how unexpectedly it rose up from the flat bare plain. More than ever it seemed to emanate mystery and strange purpose, and despite the looming storm Zluty felt its pull as he stepped into the still, damp coolness under the leaves of trees twenty times larger than the small striplings that grew by the cottage.

Zluty stood for a time listening to the leaves rustling and hissing overhead. Deeper in, the forest was silent for no wind could penetrate the dense canopy of evergreen leaves and thick interweaving branches. He loved the velvety silence there, but he liked the whispering at the outer edge of the forest, too, because he always imagined that the trees were talking to one another in some language that only trees understood; maybe speaking of his coming and wondering what he wanted.

He shook himself and began searching for the dappled bark of the trees whose sap he would tap. It was much harder spotting them in the late afternoon light than in strong morning light, so it took him a good while to find the first tree. He was pleased to see how thick its waist was, for it meant he could hammer in two tap tubes rather than one. Under each tube, he set a pot to catch the drops, making sure they stood flat so that they would not topple over as they filled.

It seemed a good omen that the first tree he had found was big enough to take two taps, for most took only one. But it took him ages to find the next tree. It turned out to be one he had used before. He knew it because there was an old tap scar in its bark. He made a new hole well above the old one, and hammered in a tube, setting another pot on the ground under it.

Just as he found a third tree, it suddenly grew dark and the redness of the light on the plain made him realise the storm cloud was now close enough to have blotted out the sun. Weariness and haste made him clumsy, and to his dismay he broke two tap tubes trying to hammer them in. The third went in properly but now he had no spare taps. He would have to be especially careful not to damage the last two.

Zluty rubbed his tired eyes and ordered himself to get on with it, for once the sun set he would be unable to see the trees well enough to know which ones to tap. He made his way back towards the outer edge of the forest where the light was stronger and, to his relief, he soon spotted another tree with dappled bark. It was easily big enough to sustain the last two taps and, elated, he very carefully hammered one in and set the second-last pot under it. But even as he shifted position to hammer in the final tap, something made him look out to the plain.

He gasped aloud to see the great wave of redness that seemed about to crash down on the forest. The storm cloud seemed to be dragging what looked like a churning shadow beneath it and he wondered if it could possibly be rain.

All at once it grew very dark and there was a great murmurous rush of wind, followed by a sound such as Zluty had never heard in his life; a thunderous tumbling roar like the noise made by the ice rain that had once fallen on the cottage roof in the early days of a hard chilly Winter, but a hundred times louder.

Zluty was puzzled but not afraid, until he saw that it was not rain or frozen ice falling, but *stones* the size of his fist. Each one slammed down so hard on the ground that it raised up a little cloud of red dust that was sucked up into the great ruddy darkness boiling overhead.

Suddenly a stone the size of his head smashed through the canopy and hit the ground not two steps away from him. Zluty staggered back, remembering how thin the outer edge of the forest canopy was. He was horrified to imagine what the stone would have done had it hit him. More horrified still to think that if he had not been in such a hurry to get back home to Bily, he might have been out on the plain now!

Bily! His heart clenched in terror at the thought of his brother enduring this impossible storm of stones, then another large stone battered its way through the canopy, shattering the pot he was still holding.

He threw down the bits of broken pottery and fled deeper into the forest until the roar of the falling stones was muted enough that he could feel sure the canopy would protect him. He told himself he was safe, but he could not stop shaking. He had got so accustomed to thinking of himself as fearless that it was an unpleasant surprise to find that something could frighten him so badly.

Zluty blundered into a fallen branch half grown over with the same thick soft moss that covered the ground under the trees, and stopped to rub his knee. He realised that if he ran on so blindly, he would surely run headlong into a tree and knock himself out. He took several deep breaths, trying to calm himself. He had no idea of how a wind could take up stones and drop them as if they were rain. It was impossible and yet it was happening.

Bily's gentle face came into his mind again, and Zluty shook his head. It was bad enough to know that his brother's lovingly tended garden must have been destroyed by the falling stones without the horror of imagining that Bily might have been outside when the stone storm came.

Zluty told himself fiercely that Bily was timid. He would not go outside when he saw the dark red clouds drawing closer. He might even have hidden under his bed!

Then Zluty thought of the warning song of the bee Queen about the earth bird. She must have meant the storm. Her dreams would have shown her the stones falling and certainly the hive would have been battered and broken if he had not covered it over with a thick layer of earth.

The muffled thunder of the stonefall went on and on, and Zluty had to accept that he could not possibly get back to the cave where his bed and his pack were while the strange storm raged overhead. The thought of spending the night in the forest without food or fire depressed him almost as much as the pot he had left sitting under the tap by the last tree, which he ought to have had the sense to grab before he fled. It would almost certainly be smashed by now.

Gradually, the darkness deepened until true night came, but the muffled rumbling of the stones went on and on and there was nothing for it but for him to lie down and try to sleep. Zluty told himself that he would still be able to leave as he had planned if he collected the mushrooms and the honey early the next day. But what if the stones went right on falling through the night and into the next day? What if the stones fell for days?

It was not long before he sat up again. Aside from feeling too unsettled to sleep, he was also cold and hungry and beginning to be thirsty again. If only he could collect mushrooms to pass the time, but he would certainly lose his way and become lost in the black depths of the forest if he tried.

Then it came to him. The collecting bag he had brought with him was part of his backpack and he was almost certain he had pushed the pouch of shining stones into one of the front pockets on the pack.

Eagerly he searched the bag and gave a cry of triumph as his fingers touched the familiar soft weave of the stone pouch.

He drew it out with trembling fingers and opened it. A soft dim light flowed up from the shining stones it contained, painting the forest grey and silver and black. The light was not strong enough to show colour.

Zluty dug some twine from his bag and wove a

net to the head of his staff, then he put the largest shining stone into it. Standing, he held the staff out before him. Its light did not travel far, but he could see a few paces in any direction. Slipping his

collection bag over his head again, Zluty turned towards the plain, and walked until he could just see the stones falling. Then he turned to the East and walked parallel to the edge of the forest until he came to the enormous boulder where he always began his journey in to the earthbank.

There were clumps of many different kinds of mushrooms growing throughout the forest, but those that grew at the earthbank were a special hardy variety that would last the trip home and retain their flavour and goodness after they had been dried.

Zluty had made his way from the boulder to the earthbank so many times that he had many markers to guide him. It was even easier now that he could see them, rather than having to grope his way from one to the other with only the distinctive scent of the earthbank mushrooms to guide him to them.

As he walked he was fascinated to see that many of the tall dark shapes he had taken for tree trunks were actually metal poles with the same mysterious markings as some of the smaller metal objects strewn about the plain. But he stopped in utter amazement to see that what he had taken

for a natural bank of earth surrounding a sunken
circle of ground was actually a great metal object
overgrown with moss and lichen. The sunken part
at the centre was a round hole in the object that

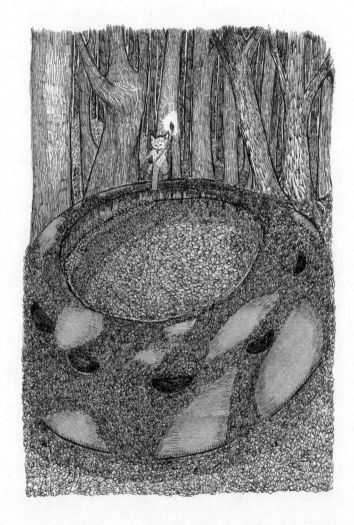

opened to the earth beneath. Zluty had never seen a metal object so large, and yet it was clear that only part of it was showing above the surface of the ground.

Zluty climbed down into the centre of it and found that the mushrooms grew as thickly as he remembered under an overhanging fringe of moss and creepers dangling from the edges of the metal object.

Thrusting his staff into the thick moss under his feet, he knelt to open his bag and get out several woven squares of cloth. Laying them out, he began to pick mushrooms, sprinkling each with earth he had brought from the cottage garden before putting it on the cloth. Once he had enough mushrooms, he tied each square into a neat bundle and set it up on the edge of the object.

It did not take him long to harvest as many mushrooms as he would be able to carry back to the cottage, and at last he stood to stretch his back, feeling stiff, and thirstier than ever. He had meant to go back to the edge of the forest when he had finished gathering the mushrooms, in the hope that the stones might have stopped falling. But now, as his eyes sought the faint greenish glow of daylight that had always before guided him back to the plain, a chill ran down his spine. He could see nothing but darkness.

Wondering if the stone in the staff was dazzling his eyes too much for him to see the dim glow of daylight, Zluty covered it with his hands. But still he could see only darkness and he remembered that it was not morning, as it usually was when he gathered mushrooms, but night, and a dark and stormy night at that.

Zluty uncovered the stone at the head of the staff and climbed up onto the object. Turning around slowly, he realised that without sunlight shining through the edges of the forest he had no idea at all of which direction he had come from. The thick moss was too springy to have left any tracks and the forest looked the same on all sides. He could try to retrace his steps from the memory of what he had seen on the way to the earthbank, but he had made that journey only once, and he had been much distracted by what he was seeing. It would be too easy to become muddled, and if he got lost and wandered deeper into the forest he would never find his way out again.

The only sensible thing was to wait for morning,

when there would be sunlight to let him see his way back to the plain.

Just so long as the stones stopped falling . . .

8

Bily stared into the little fire he had lit in the pit he had dug in the earthen floor of the cave cellar. He was thinking about the monster he had discovered the previous evening.

He glanced over to where it slept, remembering the way his heart had nearly jumped out of his chest at the sight of its glowing eyes. They were not small and bright like birds' eyes or soft and round like diggers' eyes. They were long and narrow like a grain of wild rice. And the colour – they were the light radiant yellow of the leaves that fell from the fruit trees in Autumn, and were

slashed from top to bottom by narrow black irises.

Seeing those strange eyes glaring at him out of the black shadows in the corner of the cellar, Bily had truly thought he would faint out of sheer fright. But he had not fainted and the monster had not sprung out at him and eaten him.

It had simply gone on looking at him.

Bily might very well still be standing there, frozen with terror, if the lantern had not guttered, its feeble light dimming further. Only the fear of being plunged into darkness had given Bily the strength to back away from the monster.

He had got halfway to the steps, all the while imagining how it would feel when the yellow-eyed monster leapt on him, when to his everlasting astonishment it *spoke*.

'If you go back up into your dwelling, you will die,' it had said in its thick, furry voice.

'If I stay, you will kill me,' Bily had gasped, only to distract the monster from noticing that he had taken another step back.

'I will not harm you,' said the monster. 'This is your territory and I came only because I was in need of shelter from the *arosh*.'

'What is an *arosh*?' Bily asked, horrified that there might be another monster roaming about the plain. And what must it be like if this one feared it?

'It is the red wind,' said the monster. 'The wind of stones.'

'You . . . you came here to take shelter from the storm?' Bily stammered.

'I did,' said the monster. 'Do not fear me for even if I desired to attack you, I would not be capable of it. I am hurt.'

Thinking it might be a trick to put him off-guard, Bily had asked warily, 'What is wrong with

you, monster? Were you struck by the falling stones?'

'They had not begun to fall when I smelled your dwelling. I raced across the plain with the *arosh* at my back and I had just smelled a way into this underground cavern when something bit me. It was some small creature with very sharp fangs, and its bite was very painful. Even as I broke into this under chamber, I felt my limbs failing under me. I could barely drag myself into this corner.'

Bily gave a little gasp. 'You must have stepped on a blackclaw. There is a nest of them near the digger mounds a little way from the house. Their venom causes numbness.' He had stopped, not wanting to tell the monster that whenever a digger had been bitten by a blackclaw it had suffered numbness and then it had died. But perhaps his face showed his thoughts too clearly, for the monster had given a heavy sigh.

'I should have been more careful,' it said. 'The seer told me to watch my step, but I thought he spoke only of being careful in general.'

Bily had not known what it was talking about, but the diggers always raved and rambled nonsense after being bitten.

'I can give you a lorassum leaf. It will numb the pain that will come when the venom spreads,' he offered.

'I would be grateful to have something, for pain is clawing at my belly like a beast that wishes to gnaw its way out of me,' the monster said.

Bily had been startled because usually once the pain came, a digger writhed and groaned and whimpered until Bily fed it lorassum leaf.

Bily went to where he kept his store of lorassum leaves. There were only a few left and they would no more save the monster from the deadly blackclaw venom than they had been able to save any of the diggers. But at least it would not suffer as it died. He had no idea how much leaf would be needed to soften the monster's pain, but it would need water, for the taste of the leaves was very bitter.

The lantern flame dimmed again and he hurried back to refill its reservoir. When he turned back to the monster, the brighter light showed clearly how enormous it was, and how long and sharp the claws were at the end of its four strong, long legs. But then Bily saw that the monster's golden eyes had grown cloudy, just like the diggers' eyes did when the pain was very bad towards the end.

It was this that gave him the courage to go and dipper water from one of the urns he had filled into a bowl and carry it and the lorassum leaves to the monster. As he approached it, his legs stopped of their own accord. He was two steps from the enormous triangular head, and its fangs looked long and sharp as dagger thorns against its dark muzzle.

'I can smell your fear,' the monster said softly in its thick whispering voice. A beautiful voice that, if it were a colour, would be a rich dark brown, Bily thought with the corner of his mind that was not terrified. Then he noticed that the monster was shivering and again pity overtook fear. He stepped closer and held out a lorassum leaf.

'I am not sure how much you will need. Usually, I only give the diggers half a leaf to chew, but their bodies are very small. I think you had better have a whole leaf to begin with. It will not be enough to deaden the pain completely, but I have only a few leaves, and once they run out, you will have to endure terrible pain.'

'You mean that I might not die soon enough for

the leaves to last if I have enough to numb the pain now,' said the monster.

Struck by the strange wry flash of humour in its eyes, Bily did not know what to say. The monster opened its mouth and, after a slight hesitation, Bily put the leaf into its red maw. He was surprised that neither his hand nor his voice shook as he explained to the monster that it must chew the leaf but not swallow it.

'If you swallow it, you will get a terrible belly-ache,' he warned. 'Once you have chewed it till the bitterness is gone, you must spit it out, and then you can drink some water.'

'I understand,' said the monster.

Leaving the bowl of water close enough that it had only to stretch out its head to drink, Bily went to get a rug – the diggers always complained of the cold after they were bitten. Spreading it over the monster he noticed several partly healed burned places on the pale parts of its pelt. There were also angry welts on its flank that looked fresh.

Now, gazing into the fire, Bily wondered what had caused them. It was a pity that he had not brought down the soothing salve he kept with bandages and other medicines in a little box under

his bed in the cottage, but he could not go up and try to get it until the stones stopped falling. He listened for a moment to the muted thunder of the stonefall, marvelling that he had hardly thought about the storm since discovering the monster in the cellar.

'The *arosh*,' he murmured, tasting the odd unfamiliar name and wondering why anyone would name a storm. He might have asked, but the monster had fallen into a lorassum trance so deep that it had not reacted even when he examined the bite on its swollen paw. The heat coming from the wound had told him that it would not be long before the poor monster died, and though it would not heal the hurt, he had crumbled a little of another lorassum leaf onto the bitten paw to deaden the pain before very gently binding it.

A sudden loud crash from above brought him to his feet and he stood trembling as a great shuddering and creaking ended in a rumbling series of thuds that shook the roof of the cellar, dislodging a shower of small stones. The birds screeched and flew up from the nests where he had finally got them to settle.

In the deep silence that followed, Redwing trilled to Bily that the roof of the cottage had fallen in. Bily's heart ached, but then he thought of the dying monster, and of Zluty, who might not have reached the forest in time to be safe from the red wind and the falling stones, and knew that much as he had loved it, a cottage roof could be rebuilt. A life lost was lost forever.

Bily turned to the sleeping monster and saw that although it was not asleep the lorassum had

numbed it so that it seemed not to have heard
the terrible crashing noise overhead. It lay so still
that if its eyes had not been open, he would have
thought it had died already.

Bily sat back down on the bale of white fluffs he had been using as a seat, and wondered what Zluty was doing. His brother had always been so quick-witted and clever that Bily was certain Zluty would have found a way to make himself safe, even if he had not reached the Northern Forest before the stones began to fall. It struck him all at once how very queer it was to think of the forest as a refuge, when he had thought of it as a dangerous place for so long.

Then he realised something else and sat bolt upright.

It was silent. The stones had ceased falling!

two

RAINFALL

9

Zluty was so thirsty that he kept picturing the pool in the cave, or the water shining in the well by the cottage. When he did manage to forget his thirst for a time, he worried about Bily and wondered what he would do if the stones kept falling so that it never got light enough for him to find his way out of the forest. He told himself it was silly to think the stonefall would not stop just as a rainfall did, but who knew what rules such a freakish storm would obey.

Suddenly an idea came to him of how to pass the remaining hours until morning. He could explore deeper in the forest simply by using the shining stones to mark the way from the earthbank. Of course, the stones were too few to take him far, but when he came to the end of them, he could just turn around and come back to the earthbank, collecting the stones as he went, and then strike out again in another direction.

His heart beat fast with excitement as he got up and emptied everything out of his bag but the pouch of stones and his little hammer. Slinging it over his head and shoulder, he took up his staff and carefully set one of the shining stones on the highest part of the earthbank, gouging an arrow beside it to show which direction he had first gone in. Then he set off at a measured pace, checking constantly over his shoulder to make sure he could see the shining stone. When he could only just see it, he put down another shining stone, and set off again.

He found nothing in his first journey out from the earthbank but a few bits of metal jutting up from the moss and several more of the metal tree trunks. He was surprised to find that the moss was mostly white, for he had always imagined it to be green like the moss at the edges of the forest. It was not until his third journey out that he noticed

some rare black shelf mushrooms growing from a tree. Zluty was elated. Bily especially loved them for the strong spicy flavour the tiniest piece gave a soup or stew, and they lasted almost as well as those he had gathered at the earthbank.

He picked a few and carefully folded them in leaves to carry them back to the earthbank. He was tempted to stop and try to sleep again but he decided he would make one last trip out from the earthbank, for it would be a whole year before he would be able to explore again.

He made another gouge in the moss to show which way he had gone, and set off again, wishing he would find water. He had laid down seven stones when, through the gloom, he caught sight of something that made him forget his thirst.

It was a low wall of stone, ancient and crumbled. Zluty wondered who had built it and why. Then it occurred to him that if he walked along it, he need not leave a trail of stones to show him the way he had gone. He could walk as far as the wall went! He put one stone on the wall to show where he had joined it, for the wall ran in both directions out of sight, and then he set off walking to the right, holding the staff out before him.

He had thought he might find other ancient buildings, but aside from the wall there was nothing but more enormous trees and soft moss broken only by the occasional jut of metal. Zluty counted seventy steps before the wall ended quite

suddenly at the edge of a great swathe of bare
black earth.

He put one of the shining stones on the end of
the wall and moved out onto the black earth. It

crunched loudly under his feet and some of the brittle black chunks collapsed into soft powder. Kneeling to look more closely at the ground, Zluty discovered it was not earth but charcoal and ash under his feet. A fire had burned here so blazingly hot as to scorch the very earth.

He looked up, lifting his staff high, and saw that the dense forest canopy overhead was unbroken. The branches must be sewn together by such an intricate interlacing of threads and winding creepers that they had not fallen. Was it possible the fire was so ancient that the trees had grown up around the burned space?

Zluty knew he ought to go back, but he could not resist using his remaining stones to go as far as he could across the blackened earth.

Something caught his eye a few steps away. It was a smooth round object buried under the burnt ground. He knelt and laid down his staff so that he could use both hands to dig. Then he stopped, seeing that what he had found was an egg! Not the frail pale egg of a bird or even the hard horny black egg of a lizard, but a metal egg like the one from which he had Bily had hatched – only many, many times larger!

Zluty kept digging around its edge until he found the seam. It was cracked open, the gap wide enough for him to get the head of his staff through and peer in.

Zluty's fur fluffed with shock at the sight of a white cluster of bones. Feeling ill, he realised that whatever had been inside the egg was long dead. His curiosity to know what the creature had been was stronger than the sudden fear that gripped him, and Zluty pushed the staff deeper into the metal egg. He wanted to see the shape made by the bones, but they were too big and the light of the stone too weak. Finally, he drew back and got to his feet, feeling oddly shaken.

Another glimmer of metal caught his eye. Again, he had to dig whatever it was out of the black stones, and again Zluty drew in a breath of amazed wonder. For it was another metal egg, this one small enough to fit into his hands.

He brought the head of the staff closer and studied the tiny egg. It had the same studs and seam as the enormous egg, only this one was still closed. He laid down the staff and picked it up, wondering how the eggs had got here and what they had to do with one another. Then he imagined

Bily's amazement when he saw the egg, for it was
so small and light he could easily carry it home in
the space left by the broken pots. There was no
sense in leaving it. He had no idea if the creature

inside it was alive, but if something did hatch, Bily would know how to look after it.

Thinking of Bily made Zluty long for his brother. He put the metal egg gently into his bag and turned back to the big egg. He took out his pipe and played the same solemn tune he played for the diggers when one of their number died, to mourn the enormous unknown beast that had never had the chance to live.

When the song was finished, Zluty returned to the wall, collecting the glowing stones as he went. As he walked, his thirst returned to torment him and it seemed a long time before he finally reached the earthbank. But to his great relief, even as he tucked away the last shining stone, he saw the familiar pallid greenish light of day in the distance and his heart leapt, for it meant that the long night and the deadly stonefall had both come to an end.

Eagerly, Zluty packed the mushroom bundles into his collecting bag with the metal egg and set off towards the plain. Never had he longed for anything so much as to be out in the open with nothing but the blue sky over him and sunlight warming his fur. Despite his burdens, he was almost trotting by the time he could see the plain through the gaps in the trees at the edge of the forest. The sky had a dull bruised look, but the great red cloud had vanished. The queer storm had spent itself in the night, or the wind had blown it beyond the forest to the edge of the world.

Either way, it was over.

Zluty made his way straight across the plain to the rift cave, stumbling a little over the hundreds of fallen stones. Inside the cave, he laid down his staff and bag and knelt to drink from the cool, wonderfully sweet pool of spring water. Then he stretched out on his bedroll, marvelling at his adventures. Never had so much happened on a trip to the forest. He would have to be careful how he told his tale, for he did not want to frighten Bily.

His eyes began to droop but he knew he had better trek to the forest hive to get honey and collect the pots of tree sap before he allowed himself to sleep, for he wanted to leave by dusk. If he moved quickly, there would still be time for a sleep before he left.

Returning to the forest, he was surprised at how reluctant he was to re-enter it after the long night he had just spent there. He made his way West along the outer edge of the forest until he came to the tree where the tree hive hung. He was saddened to find that it had been smashed to the ground by falling stones. There was no sign of the swarm that had inhabited it and he wondered if the bee Queen had survived. Most likely she had been killed, for being wingless she would have no way to escape. But the swarm would have taken the fledgling bee queens and that would enable them to establish a new hive. The loss of the hive would have dismayed him far more if he had not been gifted with a bee queen from the desert hive, though he was sure that in time he would locate the new forest hive.

He took enough honeycomb from the broken hive to fill the pots he had brought and then made his way back to collect the tree sap urns.

He stopped each urn with a plug of moss, pulled out the tap tubes and plugged the wounds in the trees with more moss. He was elated to discover that the urn he had left so close to the edge of the forest had survived the stonefall and was full of sap too.

Returning to the cave at midday, he stowed the urns and pots carefully in his pack, using the bundles of mushrooms to stop them banging

together. Then he made a fire and cooked some
pancakes for the journey as well as for his long
overdue supper. When he unstoppered one of the
little honey jars to use on the pancakes, the three
male bees came buzzing out of their jar, drawn by
the scent. Zluty told them about the forest hive
and they sang a song of sympathy for the doomed
Queen before taking a sample of the unfamiliar
honey to carry the memories in it back to their

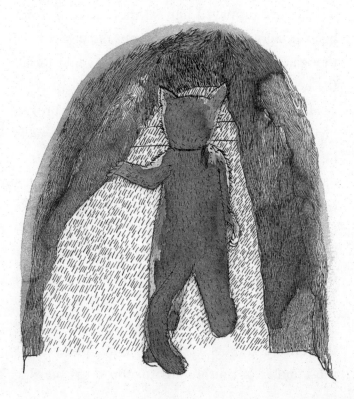

little Queen. One of the bees lingered to ask when they had got to the vale of bellflowers.

Zluty told the bee he would leave that night and if all went well they would reach the cottage early on the fourth day of travel. Once the bee had returned to its jar, Zluty cleaned his dishes and filled the water bulbs, setting them in a neat row by the pack in readiness for his departure. Only then did he stretch himself out to sleep.

He was just drifting off when he heard a loud rushing sound from outside. Feeling he had had quite enough of new things for a while, Zluty reluctantly got to his feet and went to the cave entrance.

To his astonishment, he saw that it was beginning to rain.

~ 10 ~

Bily woke from a dream of rain to find he had not been dreaming. He could hear the unmistakable sound of it falling, and knew it must be coming into the cellar through the broken trapdoor.

Sitting up, he shivered in the clammy air and wished he had not decided to wait until later to get some more ground cones from the pile behind the cottage. There was little left of the fire but glowing embers and they would soon go out if he did not feed them something to keep them alive. He thought of the basket of cones that sat beside the stove. They would be dry but he could not bring himself to go up and see the damage to the cottage just yet.

Sighing, he sat up and lit the lantern, telling himself that the rain would not last for it seldom rained on the plain for more than an hour at a time.

He thought of the monster and his heart ached with pity, for it must surely be dead. It had been racked with fever and feverish dreams the whole previous night, and nothing Bily had done had seemed to ease it. Then, midmorning, it had fallen into a deep sleep. Knowing it was unlikely to last the night, Bily had lay down himself and fallen into a deep sleep. He felt guilty at having slept while the monster died in lonely pain, and yet he had done all he could for it. He glanced up the cellar to where the monster lay and saw Redwing perched next to it on the bale of white fluffs, peering down into its face.

Bily got up and carried the lantern closer, wondering what she was doing. He was astounded to find that the monster was still breathing, though each breath was swift and shallow. It was also shivering, and seeing that the rugs he had laid

over it earlier had slipped off, Bily set the lantern
down and very gently drew them back up, then
he went back and got his own rug and laid that
over it as well.

The monster's shudders gradually eased but its eyes did not open. Bily guessed that it must be very near death. The fact that it had lived so long was astonishing, but it was clearly in terrible pain and the sooner the pain ended the better. Bily could do nothing to ease it for he had no more lorassum leaves.

He sat on a bundle of sweetgrass next to Red-wing, wondering how late it was. The storm and the rain had muddled his sense of time, but he thought it must be very early in the morning. Hesitantly, he reached out and stroked the monster's head. He had thought the darkness of its paws and muzzle were dirt, but now he saw that this was merely the way its pelt was coloured.

Without warning the monster opened its eyes a slit. Bily was enchanted all over again by their shape and hue, and thought dreamily how wonderful it would be to capture the glowing colour in a weaving or a glaze. Then he felt guilty thinking about such things when the monster was dying.

'How do you feel?' he asked, wondering if it was awake enough to hear him.

'Stiff . . . very weak,' it answered in its soft husky voice.

'I will get some more rugs,' Bily replied, marvelling that it had not spoken of its pain. He hastened off to get the old rugs he kept piled in the cellar to be used for cleaning rags. It took four rugs before the monster pronounced itself warm. Then it asked for water.

Bily carried the lantern down to get some water from one of the urns and saw that a great puddle had formed under the broken trapdoor. The rain must have been falling for some time before it had woken him. As he dippered water from the urn to a bowl, he thought how lucky it was that the cellar floor sloped down at that end, or he might have woken in a puddle of water! He shuddered at the thought for he hated to get his fur wet.

Bily carried the bowl back to the monster and trickled water as best he could into its mouth, for it was too weak to lift its head. Quite a lot ran onto the ground and soaked into the hard earth, but eventually the monster said that it had drunk enough. Bily would have liked to put some rugs under it, for the cellar floor was cold, but they had tried that earlier in the day and it had hurt the monster too much. The best he had been able to

do was to place pillows and blankets around it and under its head.

Pity assailed him and he asked it gently if there was anything else it wanted.

'Can you sing?' asked the monster.

Bily shook his head and said shyly, 'It is a pity you cannot hear my brother, Zluty. He has a little pipe he made out of reeds and you would never imagine such sweet songs as he can make with it.'

Then he had an idea. He asked Redwing if she would sing to the monster. Redwing obliged with her morning song and some of the others flitted over to join in. The monster's eyes roved over the birds, and Bily thought he saw a glimmer of humour in their glowing brightness, though he could not imagine what the monster could find funny in such a moment. Yet maybe he had been mistaken, for when the monster thanked the birds at the conclusion of their song, its voice was very grave and sincere.

The monster closed its eyes and Bily told himself there was no point putting off going outside any longer. The rain was not stopping and he would have to at least fetch the basket of ground cones, for the air in the cellar was growing colder now that the fire had all but gone out.

Trying to prepare himself for the sight of the battered cottage, he went up the cellar steps and pushed at the cellar doors to open them. To

his surprise, they would not budge. Puzzled, he pushed harder. This time red dust sifted through the gap between the two doors and he realised that some of the falling stones must have rolled over and covered them.

He climbed up another step and used his back and the strength in his legs to heave at the doors more forcefully, but no matter how he strained, they would not budge. Only then did he remember the great thunderous noise that had occurred just after he had closed the cellar doors. The roof or

part of it must have collapsed right on top of the doors! He tried once more to heave open first one and then the other, but neither gave way.

Bily went back down the steps, shuddering with distaste at the knowledge that he would have to wade through the puddle of rainwater at the other end of the cellar to find the ladder. And what if there was something wrong with the rain? Who knew how a rain that fell in the wake of a stone storm would be.

He decided he would just have to wait until the rain stopped. Surely it would not go on for much longer, and in the meantime he could burn some of the sweetgrass. There was more than enough in the cellar to fill the two new mattresses he would make once the cottage had been restored.

Carrying an armful to the fire, he threw it into the pit. There was a crackle and then a soft whoosh as the sweetgrass caught alight, and Bily sat down on his makeshift bed and relished the little flare of brightness and sweetly scented warmth.

Redwing came to sit with him and he leaned against her so he could feel the warm steady throbbing of her heart through her soft feathers. He began to think about all the things he would need to do to get the cottage back in order before Winter. Planning always comforted him, and soon he hardly heard the steady hissing sound of the rain falling and falling.

11

Zluty gazed glumly out at the falling rain. Truly this was a season of dark wonders. It was midday by his reckoning and it had been raining heavily since the previous afternoon. Worrying about the mushrooms and the bees, he had decided to wait until it stopped to set off on the journey back to the cottage. But he had never expected that the rain would go on so long.

When night came, he had tried to sleep so he would be rested enough to walk late the following night. But uneasy dreams had taken him back into the dark forest, where the enormous creature in the giant egg had come to life and had pursued him until he woke with a pounding heart, only to find it was still raining.

Now Zluty was beginning to wonder if this rain were any more natural than the stone storm had been. It had gone on for longer than any rain he had ever experienced and he had already lost most of the time he had gained in setting the taps the night he arrived. If he did not leave soon, he would not even reach the cottage by nightfall on the tenth day.

Zluty clenched his teeth and thrust his hand out into the rain. When it did not hurt him, he forced himself to step out into it, gasping a little at the pummelling it gave his sensitive ear tips. It was very heavy rain and in seconds his fur was completely soaked. The feeling of being so wet was horrible but it was only water.

He splashed across to the forest to get some leaves and carried them back to the cave, noticing that the red stones which had fallen were beginning to dissolve and soften.

He got a thorn needle and some thread from his pack and sewed the leaves together, then he bound them to his staff to make a parasol that would keep the rain off his pack. Lashing it in place, he settled the bee jar into it and pushed a little moss loosely into the top of it to make sure no rain would drip inside. Then, with a last glance around the cave, he shouldered the pack, slung the collection bag over his head and set off.

So much rain had fallen that the ground was too sodden to absorb it. Great pools had formed, full of widening and overlapping ripples, and in between the pools the ground was soft and slimy from the dissolving sludge of the storm stones. But Zluty hardly noticed the wet or the cold or the slippery muddy ground.

He was going home.

It was afternoon when Zluty noticed a sodden digger standing up on its haunches. No doubt it had scented his approach for diggers had very keen noses. Coming closer, he noticed that the little creature's fur was quite a different colour to that of the diggers that lived near the cottage.

'Ra!' it cried in greeting, blinking rain from its eyes.

'Ra,' Zluty responded. 'Where did you come from?'

In answer, the digger beckoned and splashed
away to the East where it vanished over a low rise
of ground.

Zluty hesitated. He was anxious to get home,
but he was curious what it could want of him and

in truth he was weary enough from his dreary trudge to welcome a diversion.

When he got to the top of the rise, he saw that there was a little delegation of diggers awaiting him, their fur plastered flat by the rain. Zluty bowed to them and asked if they had some need of him.

The digger that had led him to the others nodded passionately and then an older digger explained with a few words and a goodly amount of gesturing and miming that its clan was hungry because rain had got into their burrow system. Zluty asked in dismay if their food store had been destroyed, knowing this would mean the difference between survival and death on the barren plain.

The diggers gave a chittering giggle until the speaker quelled them with a severe look. Turning back to Zluty, he explained that the food storage was almost certainly dry because it was higher than the rest of the burrow, but it could only be reached by a long deep tunnel that had been flooded and had collapsed. The diggers only needed enough food to tide them over until they could dig a new tunnel to the store.

Zluty was relieved and said he could give them some food. He was about to take off his pack but the speaker urged him to come and eat with the clan.

'I will not fit into a digger burrow,' Zluty said, but the speaker managed to convey to him that

the clan had taken refuge in a place that was big enough for him to join them.

Zluty asked where it was, but he could not understand what the digger tried to tell him. Finally, he simply gestured them to lead the way. If they had found some place where he could get out of the rain, he would be glad to rest for a while and eat something, for he had not stopped since setting out.

The diggers brought him to a ground cave with such a small entrance that Zluty had to push his pack and his other burdens in first, then crawl in after them. But it was a great relief to be out of the relentless rain. The diggers called him to come deeper. When he obeyed he was pleased to find that the cave widened out, so that he could sit up.

Now that he was not walking, he had begun to feel cold and he decided to light a fire and make a stew of mushrooms to share with the diggers. They did not traditionally cook their food, but the ones in the burrow near the cottage had liked anything Bily and Zluty offered. He set about finding a dip in the rocky cave bottom that would serve as a fire pit and laid his last three ground cones into it. He tore up some white fluffs, and struck his flint stones over them. A little spark fell and a thread of smoke curled up. He leaned nearer and blew the spark until the cones caught alight.

Zluty sat back in satisfaction only to see that the little diggers had drawn back in fright. Realising they had only ever seen wild fire before, he made soothing gestures and tried to assure them that these flames were in his control, but he did not have Bily's gentle skill at communicating with the little creatures and they continued to regard the flames with alarm.

Zluty turned back to the fire and propped a pot over it and filled it with mushrooms and various herbs and the water from one of his bulbs. He would normally have been more careful with his water supply, but with so much rain falling it was hard to feel worried about running out.

The fire soon warmed the cave and the scent of the mushrooms cooking was delicious. The diggers might never have tasted cooked food, but the smell must have been pleasing to them, for eventually they crept forward, their eyes shining hungrily. Zluty poured some of the stew into his bowl for them when it was ready, and ate his own share out of the pot.

The diggers were still eating when he finished, so he got out his little pipe and played them a tune. The diggers at the cottage had always liked the songs he made with the pipe, and these diggers were no different. They listened with rapturous attention until he set the pipe aside, and then they made the same chittering sound of appreciation as the other diggers always did.

Zluty thanked them and only then noticed that several of the younger diggers had been rummaging in his pack. They had got out the small metal egg and were crooning and stroking it. Zluty smiled, knowing how diggers loved to collect shiny things. The ones near the cottage were always dragging home smaller bits of metal to decorate their burrows.

Deciding they would do it no harm, Zluty checked on the bees to make sure they had not been disturbed. He knew he ought to go, but the rain was still falling steadily and it was a pity to waste the fire. He stretched himself out with a sigh.

His last sight was of a cluster of little diggers gazing gravely and worshipfully into the fire, the metal egg gleaming in their midst.

As he slept, a memory came to Zluty of the time after he and Bily had emerged from their egg. They had been small and very helpless, but the egg had been filled with food, and voices inside their heads had told them about the spring, and had explained how to build a shelter from the egg. They had obeyed the inner voices and had lived in the egg house until they grew too large to fit into it. Then the voices told them they must build a new, larger cottage out of things from the plain.

When at length they had run out of the egg food, the inner voice told Zluty of the wild rice and the roots that could be dug from the ground, but it warned that this food would not feed them through the Winter that would come. Before that season, Zluty must go North to a great forest where he could find other foodstuffs.

Zluty put the journey to the Northern Forest off for a long time because the voice inside Bily's head said nothing about a forest or a journey, and his brother had looked frightened whenever Zluty spoke of going there to search for food to supplement their supplies. But the inner voice had been insistent and finally Zluty decided he must go before it was too late. Perhaps the voice had whispered something to his brother, too, for when he told Bily what he meant to do, Bily had not argued.

In his dream, Zluty saw himself leaving Bily that first time, setting off across the plain too close to Winter, with too little water and no idea of how near he would come to dying. Then the dream faded and there was only a voice whispering urgently to Zluty that he must go before it was too late.

Zluty woke in the stale smoke-scented darkness of the digger cave to find the diggers were asleep all around him in little furry piles. The pale grey light of pre-dawn was filtering through the entrance at the other end of the cave, and he could hear that it was still raining, but the memory of the whispered warning that had woken him would not let him go back to sleep.

He swiftly repacked his flints and the pot licked clean by the diggers, wondering if the voice had spoken to him after all this time. It had once whispered constantly to him, telling him to do certain things, advising him what sorts of food could be safely eaten, but he had not heard it for many long years.

He had come very close to dying on that first trip to the Northern Forest. This was one of the reasons Bily feared his trips there. Yet their lives had been so much improved by the things Zluty had brought back, that they had both known he would make the trip again. Of course, the next time Zluty had known what to expect and he had been far better prepared. He had not needed the voice. Maybe that was why it had fallen silent.

It might just be the wrongness of stones falling from the sky and the unnatural rain that had awakened a memory of the voice, but when he thought of the words it had said, the fur on his neck and ears bristled.

Go, before it is too late.

He rose quietly, and lifted the metal egg from between two sleeping diggers, being careful not to wake them. On impulse, he got one of the shining stones from its pouch and put it between them where the egg had been, wondering what the little creatures would make of his gift. The egg was still warm from the body heat of the diggers when he pushed it gently into the depths of his pack alongside the bee jar. He took out the pancakes he had cooked the previous night, and put them in a pile by the burned-out fire pit so that the diggers would have something to eat when they woke, then he crawled back to the entrance of the cave, dragging his pack and the collection bag after him.

Outside, the rain immediately began seeping through his fur, but he ignored it as he arranged the staff and leaf parasol to protect the mushrooms and the bee jar.

'Perhaps when dawn comes the rain will stop,' he told himself as he set off.

12

Bily sat up in dismay, realising he had fallen asleep waiting for the rain to cease. The fire was now utterly dead, the embers black and lifeless. He could see only because it was morning, though it was a dreary grey morning and still the rain fell. He sat up and gasped aloud to see that the dark puddle under the broken cellar doors had spread so that almost half the cellar was now under water.

Bily leapt up and dragged his bedding further up the cellar floor before going to check on the monster. He was worried that it might have lost

its blankets again, for the air was cold and clammy
with dampness, but instead, as he approached it, he
felt a terrible sick heat coming from its body.

He lit the lantern so that he could examine its
bitten paw and was horrified to see it had swollen
to twice its proper size. He soaked some of the
white fluffs in the bowl of water he had left by its
head, and spread them over the monster's hot face
and neck to try to cool it down. The fluffs weighed

almost nothing but the pain of the wound must have been awful, for the monster groaned and gnashed its teeth when Bily lay one of them on the wound. Suddenly its eyes flew open. They blazed with feverish brightness.

'I should have been more careful . . .' it said. 'I should not have been so clever, thinking I could change things that have been unchanged for thousands of years . . . Cleverness will . . . will be the death of me.'

Bily said nothing, for he saw that the monster was not truly awake. Its eyes were wild and it shifted restlessly in the grip of some fever dream. He left it to drag everything that was still dry up to the high end of the cellar. Last of all, he carried the birds' nests to the shelves near the monster, where he kept his seed cases, for that was the last place the water would reach. Then he tried again to force open the cellar doors. They were as immovable as ever.

He came slowly back down the steps, feeling sick, for there was only one thing he could do now. He must wade out into the water under the broken trapdoor, find the ladder and climb out of the cellar so that he could get the stones off the other doors. He had to do it now for if the water kept on rising it would eventually fill the cellar. He could save himself and the birds by climbing out of the cellar, but the only way the monster would be able to get out was to climb the steps and come out the cellar doors. He refused to think about the fact that the monster was too weak even to lift its own head. The longer it lived, the more determined he became that he would save it.

Bily stopped at the edge of the pool of water. It was so much deeper than it had been. Down by the end wall where the ladder had fallen, it would probably reach up to his neck.

He hated getting wet above anything. He had sometimes had nightmares about Zluty wading into the black filthy water of the swamp, but even his brave brother had never got into water as deep as this.

Bily told himself that it was his own fault for having put it off for so long. If he had gone the night before instead of deciding to wait until the rain stopped, it would be over with. He wished with all his heart that Zluty would come and save them, but Zluty would only just have left the Northern Forest that morning. If he had not delayed because of the rain and if he had not been hurt by the falling stones, it would still take him four days to get home.

At least now there was daylight he would be able to see the ladder. He shuddered anew at the realisation that he would have to put his head under the water to look for it, and forced himself to step into the water. It reached through his warm fur and touched his skin like hundreds of cold little fingers. Bily stopped, shuddering with disgust and fear.

'I have to do it,' he told himself.

Only then did he notice Redwing, perched on the top of one of the water jugs and watching him with her small bright eyes. She gave a chirp of enquiry, but he did not know how to explain what he meant to do without also telling her how frightened he was. So he just smiled at her and forced himself to take another step into the icy black water.

As he moved forward, the feel of the water creeping through his thick belly fur was far more horrible than he had imagined it would be, but he clenched his teeth and told himself that when at last all of this strangeness was long past and they sat by the fire and talked of this time, for once

his stories would be more dramatic and exciting than Zluty's.

The water was now at his chest, but he hesitated for his breath had caught in his throat and would not go in or out. He forced himself to take another step forward and gasped at the feel of the water creeping up under his arms. A little whimper of fear came from him because he was still several steps from the end of the cellar and if he took one more step his head would go under the water.

'I have to put my head under to find the ladder,' he reminded himself desperately. He was at the very edge of the uneven square of light coming down through the broken doors, and tiny drops of water were splashing up into his face from the force of the falling raindrops.

He closed his eyes and thought of Zluty, then he stepped forward. The water came up to his mouth and as he lifted his head he felt the rain falling on his ears and head. Gasping in a final breath of air, he took another step and went under.

The silence was immediate and absolute, and the feeling of water against his eyes and in his ears was very strange. Bily looked around. The light was very dim and slightly greenish-yellow under the murky water. He tried to bend down but the water resisted him, slowing his movement and making him awkward. His feet floated up and this frightened him, but he forced himself to stay calm and pushed against the water to make himself go forward.

At last he could see the cellar floor. He had hoped to see the ladder at once, but instead he saw only a shadow some distance away. He flapped and pushed and struggled against the water until he was close enough to see that it was only a piece of wood that had broken off from the trapdoor. But just past it lay the ladder, broken into pieces.

Then Bily saw something else. It was so strange
and unexpected that for a moment he forgot his
dismay at seeing the ladder was broken and his
loathing of being wet. It was a crack running along

the floor of the cellar and up the end wall. Bily came close enough to catch hold of the edges of the crack and that was when he felt the distinctive flow of icy-cold water against his face.

Fear filled him at the realisation that water was flowing into the cellar. Bily did not know how that could be, but he needed to breathe badly now. He let go of the crack and tried to stand up, but he had forgotten that the water was too deep here for him. Beginning to panic, he thrashed and flailed forwards, desperate to get his head above the water. But as soon as he moved away from the wall, he lost his sense of direction. He ought to have been able to work out which way to go from the slope of the floor, but the water was confusing his senses and his feet kept trying to float up.

He fought for calmness. His ears ached and his chest burned with the need to breathe, but still he could not think which way to go.

'I am going to drown,' he thought despairingly.

Then he heard a muffled splash. He looked up and was astonished to see red feathers. With a rush of love and relief he realised it was Redwing, flapping overhead and trying to show him which way to go. He watched until he saw the feathers break

the water again, a little further away, and then he pushed his hands against the water as hard as he could, propelling himself in that direction.

Bily's ears emerged from the water so that he could hear Redwing piping her distress overhead. He tilted his head back and stood on tiptoes to draw a breath of air, then he pushed himself forward again. At last he was high enough to get his head properly above the water.

Bily felt drained of all strength, but he floundered

his way slowly to dry ground. He was so weakened by his ordeal that he could only crawl above the water line, then he lay down, gasping. He would have fallen asleep like that but Redwing landed beside him, nudging and pricking at him with her beak until he gave into her urging and crept up to his bedding. But there were no blankets, for he had given them to the monster.

Shuddering with cold, he staggered up to where the monster slept, muttering and grinding its fangs, and curled up beside its fevered body. Redwing snuggled as close as she could on the other side of Bily to try and warm him.

It was some time before Bily realised that he could no longer hear the sound of the falling rain. The fact that it had stopped at last ought to have cheered him, but Bily could only think of the force of the water he had felt flowing so strongly into the cellar through the crack in the floor. They would drown unless he could figure a way to get out of the cellar.

three

HEARTFALL

13

Not long after the rain ceased, the clouds began to fray and disperse. First there was blue sky and then the sun came out. It transformed the great grey puddles of water into dazzling pools of gold and silver and the world became so radiantly beautiful that it took Zluty's breath away.

He walked all that day and deep into the night, keeping up a fast pace for he was determined to reach the cottage as soon as he could. He stopped near morning only because he found a little cluster of dry ground cones caught in a tiny rift that allowed him to light a fire. He would not have stopped at all, but walking in the cold and the rain had given him a chill and he did not want it to get any worse. He made himself some soup and though he had not intended to sleep, being full and warm made him drowsy. Before he knew it he was dreaming that he was setting off on a bright day to dig for tubers, dragging his wheeled pallet after him. As he walked, the pallet grew heavier and heavier until finally he turned around to see if something had got tangled around the wheels. He saw with a thrill of horror that the bones from inside the enormous metal egg were lying on it, gleaming with a ghastly whiteness in the sun.

Then the bones spoke to him in a hissing sibilant voice. '*Hurryyyy.*'

The nightmare brought Zluty wide-awake with a thundering heart. After he had gotten over the fright, he was glad the nightmare had woken him and kept him from sleeping half the day away. He was much better for the food and rest, and the chilly ache had gone from his bones. If only he did not feel so anxious for Bily. The more he thought about the inner voice that had whispered at him to hurry, the more sure he was that it had not been a dream; the more sure he was that Bily was in danger.

He was glad of the distraction when the bees emerged to buzz about his ears, asking when they had got to the vale of bellflowers. He had taken the moss stopper from their urn when he had thrown away the limp leaf parasol.

'This afternoon or tonight,' he promised them, wondering how any of the bellflowers could have survived the stonefall.

A little later they came to a slope he recognised as being less than half a day from the cottage. A wild crop of feathergrass had once grown on the other side of the slope, but it was so badly crushed and mired over with wet, red mud that he doubted the plants would ever manage to reseed. That made him wonder how the wild rice in the swamp and the white fluff plants had fared. Wild crops were hardy, but the battering the plain had taken during the stonefall was not something they would ever have experienced before. He wondered for the hundredth time what had caused the strange storm, but knew he was no more likely to learn the answer to that question than to discover what the creature was that had died in the enormous egg he had found in the Northern Forest. The world was full of mysteries and secrets that cared nothing for his curiosity.

Bily thought that a mystery was pointless unless it could be solved, but Zluty had always liked imagining that the world was full of mysteries no one would ever solve. Yet somehow, the stone storm had shaken his delight in unknown things.

It was almost dusk when Zluty came at last to the top of a familiar rise and looked down the other side. His eyes searched hungrily for the cottage in its hollow, but there was nothing. Where the cottage ought to have been was a ruin of rubble and broken boards. There was only one part of the wall left standing. The lovely garden Bily had planted and nurtured was completely gone, most of it swallowed up by a great pool of reddish-brown water that lapped up against the remaining wall.

But where was Bily?

Zluty had to force his fingers to unhook themselves from his staff so that he could take off his pack and his collection bag. He ran down the slope towards the destroyed cottage. Then he stopped. His heart beat with a strange and dreadful apprehension as he gazed at what had once been the

door to his home. The great branches that he had dragged in his wheeled cart from the Northern Forest to serve as the main beams and lintels were broken and half buried under rubble. He thought of the long, back-breaking hours he and Bily had spent gathering and mortaring stones into what had become the strong outer walls of the cottage. The kitchen table had been entirely flattened beneath one of the roof beams, along with one chair, and the other chair lay on its side with two legs snapped off.

The only thing that seemed undamaged was the stone oven in which Bily had made so many pies and loaves of bread. It stood, squat and solid and unharmed in the midst of the chaos. Zluty stared at it, thinking of how many Winter nights he and Bily had sat before it warming themselves as he had played on his pipe.

Sorrow welled up in Zluty and he sat down in the midst of the ruins and wept. All of the joy he had taken in setting off on his annual journey to the forest seemed a dreadful mockery now, for what did any adventure mean in the face of such a terrible loss?

'Bily,' he sobbed. 'Oh, Bily, I am so sorry I was not here to help you.'

14

It was a long time before Zluty could bear to get up and begin the search for his brother's body, which he knew must be buried under the rubble. The thought of finding Bily and of having to kiss his cold face and bury him was so awful that Zluty sobbed until he could hardly see out of his tear-swollen eyes.

He had only just begun to haul rocks aside to get at the table, weeping anew at the horrible vision that came to him of his brother hiding under it as the roof fell, when he thought he heard something.

He froze and listened, fur fluffed out with the

urgency of the hope that suddenly burned in his heart. Then, all at once, Zluty realised something that he had been too distraught to think of sooner. Bily must have taken refuge in the cellar!

Heart pounding, Zluty began frantically to lift away the great mound of stones that covered the cellar doors. Some of the rocks were still mortared together and were too heavy to lift, so he rolled them aside.

Fear and hope and weariness had muddled together in his mind and were making it very hard to think clearly. So it was that he had been labouring for some minutes before he remembered the outer entrance to the cellar. If Bily had been inside the cellar and unable to open the doors at the top of the steps leading into the cottage, he would simply have climbed up the ladder to get out the other door. If he had not done so, it must be because he could not, which meant he must be injured!

Zluty hastened to climb over the broken section of the cottage wall to get to the outer cellar doors, but with a rush of despair he saw that the dark pool of water he had seen from the top of the slope had covered the doors completely.

Zluty gave a cry of anguish and returned to the

inner cellar doors, frantically shifting stones and telling himself that the cellar could not be completely flooded. There must be space where there was air to breath.

But there were so many stones! Zluty worked, refusing to allow himself to dwell on it any more until at last he had cleared enough of the rubble to see the wooden doors.

'Bily!' he shouted.

He strained his ears to hear the slightest sound, but there was nothing save the terrified banging of his own heart.

With renewed desperation, he pushed and levered and struggled to shift some more stones until at last he had exposed the seam between the two doors. He stopped his mad assault at once, seeing that both doors were cracked and buckling under the weight of two clusters of stone that had formed into enormous boulders. One rested squarely on each door, and they leaned heavily against each another. Even if he managed to move one, the other one would topple forward and smash through the doors.

Zluty felt sick with fear at the thought that his brother might even now be under the doors, unable to speak, and unable to retreat because of the water filling the cellar. Oh, for a moment he was so frightened for Bily that he just knelt there trembling. But then he gathered his courage and ran back up the hill to get his staff. It was very strong wood and it would make a good lever. Returning, he was casting about for smaller stones or bits of metal that he could use as wedges, when he heard a muffled thud.

He stopped and listened.

Thud! He heard it again. But he also heard a woody creak from the overburdened cellar doors.

'Bily!' Zluty shouted. 'Get back from the doors!'

This time he thought he heard a muffled shout.

He pushed a small stone against the base of the lesser boulder, then he used the staff to lever it up just enough to allow him to push the thin end of a wedge under it with his foot. He let the boulder down gently and was relieved when the wedge held. He did the same to the other boulder so that neither would roll forward if he moved the other. He went back to the first boulder and again pushed the tip of his staff under it. He heard another thump from below, but he did not dare answer for his whole being was concentrated on holding the unwieldy rock cluster steady so that he could push in a second, larger wedge.

Once he was sure the wedge was steady he got a third wedge. Gradually, in this way, he forced the boulder back until it was resting against the cellar door frame. His fur was dripping with sweat and his muscles were trembling, but all he had to do now was to get the boulder up onto the rim of the frame, then he could use the staff to tip it backwards.

But he had to rest for a bit.

Zluty lay down on the ground and put his eye to the slit between the doors.

He could see only darkness through it. He put his mouth against the door and called his brother's name, then he put his ear to the slit.

'Zluty?' A voice rasped.

It was Bily.

Zluty lay his head on the ground, for the relief he felt at hearing his brother's voice was so power-ful that it had stolen all the strength from him. Before he could bring himself to speak, he heard the scratchy whisper again.

'Zluty, you have to get us out of here. The cellar is full of water and it's still coming in.'

'Get back,' Zluty said, whispering too, though

there was no reason for it. 'I am shifting the stones out of the way so I can open the cellar door. But the wood is cracked and if these great boulders on top of it fall through . . .' he stopped and waited, but there was no response save for the sound of something moving through water.

Zluty got to his feet, took up his staff and set the tip against the boulder again. Hearing Bily talk had heartened him. He shoved the staff deep under the balanced boulder, put his shoulder to it and heaved with all his might.

For one moment nothing happened, then the door creaked horribly and the boulder was falling slowly backwards.

Zluty dropped to his knees and set the staff aside. His whole body was aching as he reached out and tried to open the door, but it was stuck fast because it had buckled and jammed against the frame. He gave a gasping sob of frustration, until he saw that the door was being pushed from below.

'Careful!' Zluty cried, alarmed that the wedge under the other boulder would shift. 'We have to get this door open without moving the other one. There is another big bit of the wall on it . . .'

Bily said nothing, but this time instead of pushing at the door he pulled. There was a splintering crack and one of the boards broke in half. An explosion of feathers and claws erupted from the gap.

'Zluty, quickly!' Bily urged.

Zluty knelt and looked through the broken door. Bily's filthy face looked up at him, his soft white fur smeared with dirt and completely saturated. Zluty knew how much his neat brother loathed being wet, but Bily hardly seemed aware of the state of his fur and face for he was pushing a nest with

several eggs in it up through the gap. Zluty had no
more set it aside than Bily was passing up another
nest, this one with a clutch of little nestlings in it.

Then there was another and another until Zluty understood that Bily must have brought all of the nests from the garden down into the cellar, and convinced the adult birds to take refuge there as well, before the stones began to fall.

'That was the last one,' Bily said. 'Oh, Zluty! I don't know how you can be here so soon but thank goodness you are!'

'I hurried,' Zluty said, reaching through the gap to take his brother's hand and squeeze it. But how cold it was! He began pulling at another of the boards in the broken door, keeping a wary eye on the boulder balanced on the other door. Once the second board was freed, he could see better. Black water lapped more than halfway up the steps and Redwing was sitting on the step beside Bily, for she was too large to fit through the opening. Zluty began to work on freeing another board with renewed but careful energy.

'Once I get this next one free, you and Redwing should be able to fit through,' he panted.

But Bily shook his head. 'No, Zluty. We have to get both doors open so that the monster can get out.'

Zluty stared at his brother, wondering if the falling board had struck him on the head.

'Monster?' he repeated.

'Hurry!' Bily urged.

Zluty saw the stubborn desperation in his brother's face and knew there was no use arguing with him. He was very tired, but he forced himself to rethink the problem of the doors. Finally, he put his face back to the gap and said, 'The second boulder is too big for me to roll away. The only thing I can do is push it forward and let it fall into the cellar. I think it will just smash through the doors but you have to get right back out of the way.'

Zluty expected Bily to argue that he could not go back without getting wet, but instead his timid brother simply said again, 'Hurry!' before turning and scooping Redwing into his arms and backing down the steps into the water. He vanished in the shadows and, after a long moment, Bily shouted out to him in a muffled voice to let the boulder fall.

Zluty set aside the remarkable behaviour of his brother and stood. He took up his staff again. He was totally exhausted now and this boulder was much bigger than the other was, but at least this time all he had to do was lever it up, kick the wedge out of the way and let it fall forward. The weight of it would smash through both doors and then it would fall into the cellar and down the steps.

The whole thing took but a moment, yet as the massive boulder toppled forward Zluty's heart leapt into his throat at the sudden fear that it might jam in the opening. But it crashed through the cracked cellar doors and landed with a resounding thud onto the top step before toppling ponderously down to the next step, and the next, to be swallowed up by the murky water.

'Bily?' Zluty called into the darkness.

'Come down!' Bily's voice floated eerily back to him.

Puzzled that his brother did not simply come back up the stairs, Zluty climbed down the cracked steps to the step above the water. Now he could see that everything in the cellar had been piled at the upper end of the sloping floor. Bily must have done it when the water first began to rise, never imagining that the water would come so high.

'Hurry,' Bily urged. His voice came from behind the piled-up mass and Zluty stifled a sigh and stepped down into the water with a grimace. The cold wetness crept through his fur, but at least it was not the thick black mud of the swamp. He had climbed down two more steps before it occurred to him that if he went to the bottom, the water would be over his head! However had Bily got across the cellar?

'Jump off the side rather than down the proper way,' Bily called, his head showing above a sodden bale of white fluffs. 'It's not so deep there.'

Zluty wanted to tell Bily to come out of the cellar and they would light a fire and dry out before they worried about the supplies. But no doubt it was worrying about them that had kept Bily from panicking, and it was true that they would need whatever they could salvage from the cellar. Zluty took a deep breath and jumped from the side of the steps into the water.

He gave a cry of alarm to find that the water came right up to his chest! He could hardly believe Bily had told him to jump into it, but he must have done it himself already. Hardly able to imagine his timid brother wading through such deep dark water, he moved slowly towards the shallow end of the cellar.

When he was closer, he saw that what he had taken for a pile of things was actually a barrier keeping the water back from the top part of the cellar. Bily must have built it to keep some of the supplies in the cellar safe, or perhaps to provide himself with a dry place to sit. When Zluty got to the barrier, the water was only up to his knees. He looked over the barrier and saw that Bily was bending over what appeared to be a great pile of blankets between the pallet and the wall.

Zluty opened his mouth to ask what he was doing, and then froze as the pile of blankets

moved. Now he saw that under them lay an enormous beast with a long snaky tail and claws that glimmered sharphy in the lantern light.

'What is it?' Zluty gasped, through lips that felt numb and cold.

'Don't be frightened,' said Bily. 'It is only the monster.'

'Only,' Zluty echoed faintly.

Bily bade him climb over the barrier, and when Zluty had done so, his brother explained how the monster had been fleeing the red wind when it was bitten by a blackclaw and had taken refuge in the cellar. Although it had miraculously survived the bite until now, it was fevered and very weak.

Zluty could feel the heat coming from the monster, and he guessed it was its size that had kept Bily's monster alive this long.

'We just need to get it onto the wheeled pallet so that we can float it up the stairs,' Bily concluded eagerly.

Zluty stared at his brother blankly. 'How do you know the pallet will float?'

'The egg it's made from will float and the wood will hold it up too,' Bily said.

There was a pleading note in his voice that forced Zluty to pull his scattered wits together. He turned to look at the monster. 'Exactly how much of it is there under those blankets?'

'Quite a lot, but most of it is fur,' Bily assured him.

Zluty wanted to tell Bily it would be kinder to let the poor monster lie in peace until it died. But he said, 'I will go see if the pallet will fit through the doors. I can float it over here but we will have to get the monster onto it before we take away the barricade and float it to the steps. We will have to drag it the last bit of the way up though, so we will have to tie it on.'

'That will hurt it terribly,' Bily said worriedly. 'If only I had some lorassum leaf left.'

For some reason, Zluty found himself thinking of the enormous bones of the creature in the metal egg that had never got a chance to live, but he said nothing about that, instead he told Bily that he had a lorassum leaf in his pack.

'We can give some to the monster before we move it, only I don't know how we will manage to get it onto the pallet in the first place. Can it move at all?'

He glanced at the monster and was unnerved to find its glowing yellow eyes were now open and fixed on him.

'Not usefully,' it answered in a voice as thick and smooth as tree sap. There was pain in its words, but Zluty thought there was amusement in his tone, too. Yet surely he had imagined that, for how could any creature be amused at such a moment?

'This is my brother that I told you about, Monster,' Bily said. His head was so close to the monster's maw that it could have bitten it off. He turned back to Zluty. 'It doesn't matter if it can't help. We can just drag it onto the pallet using its fur.'

'Drag it by its fur?' Zluty repeated, wincing at the thought of being lifted up by his fur. He went back out of the cellar to get the lorassum leaf. The sun had set, but there was still a reddish smear of light in the West so it must have only just gone down. A few stars were beginning to glitter over-head and soon the moon would rise.

Zluty resisted the desire to linger in the fresh air and went back down into the cellar to give the lorassum leaf to Bily, then he went out again to find the wheeled pallet. It lay under a great tangle of sodden roof tiles and when he had got it free, he dragged it into the ruin of the cottage and down to the cellar.

Luckily, the opening was wide enough for it to fit through, and despite its size, the pallet was easy to move because the metal eggshell was very light. When he got the pallet into the water, it floated just as Bily had said it would, and between them they got it over the barrier.

Bily immediately grasped two thick handfuls of the monster's pelt with complete disregard for its deadly claws and sharp white teeth and urged Zluty to do the same. Zluty had to remind himself that the monster was barely able to move before he could bring himself to obey. The monster's fur was remarkably soft and he had to wind his fingers into it to get a good grip.

'Ready?' Bily asked.

Zluty swallowed and nodded and between them they heaved and tugged until they had got the monster onto the pallet. It had been heavy but not nearly as heavy as Zluty had expected. It did not once complain that they were hurting it, and Zluty wondered if it was the lorassum leaf, or the numbness that sometimes happened just before death that stopped it feeling pain. It would be awful to have the monster die as they were moving it.

He forced himself to stop thinking about what might happen as he set about tying ropes onto the pallet to secure the monster to it. Meanwhile, Bily was dismantling the barrier.

'Now we will see if it floats,' he said.

He was talking to the monster, and Zluty tried to imagine how his brother had come to befriend it. But he only said, 'If the pallet does not float under your weight, Monster, you will have to hold your breath until we can haul you up the steps.'

'Very well,' said the monster, sounding more wearily resigned than frightened.

They turned the pallet so that its head was facing the steps, and pulled it deeper into the water. It sank under the weight of the monster a good deal, but stayed high enough in the water to make it clear that they would be able to float it across the cellar to the steps.

Zluty had thought to cut the monster free of the pallet and pull it out of the cellar, but now he saw it would be easier to leave the monster on it for it had fallen unconscious. He found some flat bits of wood to make a ramp and wound the ropes around the stove and the remaining section of the wall for leverage, then he and Bily pulled until the pallet had emerged from the cellar and stood dripping in the midst of the ruined cottage.

The moon had now risen and Zluty sank down in utter exhaustion and relief, but Bily looked around at the mess and burst into tears.

⟅ 15 ⟆

Bily had brought out the small honey cakes he had managed to save, giving two to Zluty to serve for their supper and soaking the third in water. He smeared the sweet slime onto the monster's swollen paw in the hope of drawing some of the swelling and poison from the blackclaw bite, having decided that it was better to do it while it slept in a lorassum dream.

Redwing and some of the other birds came to peck at the crumbs he dropped. Watching them, Bily thought with a pang of his ruined seed collection. Some of the seeds might be saved, but there would be no way to tell if they were still good other than by planting them to see what happened. The thought of planting anything made him think about his precious garden and that made him feel sad and a little sick. Better to concentrate on trying to heal the monster.

It had been Zluty's suggestion to leave it on the pallet, since that was warmer than the ground. Not that the monster needed warming. The heat of its fever was so great now that the parts of its fur that had got wet as they brought it out of the cellar were almost dry.

He bandaged the paw loosely about the mess of honey cake and then tried to trickle some water into the monster's mouth, but it just dribbled out again. Giving up, Bily set the bowl by the monster, propping it so that it had only to turn its head to drink. Though he was not sure if the poor thing had the strength even for that. He knew very well that Zluty believed it would die and even the monster thought so. Part of Bily feared they were right, but a small stubborn bit of him refused to accept it. Why would the monster have lasted so long if it was only going to die?

He lingered, gazing into its face, but there was

nothing more he could do for it. He looked up the
slope to where Zluty had set up a makeshift camp,
and was even now cooking them some soup. Neither of them had wanted to camp right beside the
ruined cottage, and besides, the water in the cellar
was still rising.

Bily knew that Zluty was waiting for him, but he
did not like to leave the monster alone. If only they

could have brought the pallet up the hill, but the ground sloped too much for it to be safe.

Finally Bily leaned close to the monster and whispered into its dark furred ear, 'Please don't die.'

The monster stirred and Bily thought it would open its eyes, but it did not.

'I will watch over him,' Redwing promised.

Bily heaved a sigh and made his weary way up the slope to the fire. Halfway there, he could smell that Zluty was frying mushrooms. He felt faint with hunger.

Zluty smiled at him across the fire, the waves of heat causing him to waver and blur like a vision. For a moment, Bily thought he was dreaming, and that he must still be trapped in the cellar.

'Sit down,' Zluty commanded gently. 'You will feel better once you have some mushrooms inside you.'

Bily sat down on the folded blanket his brother had indicated and held his hands out to the flames. Zluty had often told him how nice it was to be sitting by a fire under the open sky, but Bily had always preferred being inside the cottage by his little stove. Only now the stove was outside as well, he thought sadly.

Zluty pushed a plate of mushrooms into his hands and ordered him sternly to eat. Underneath the bossiness Bily could hear his brother's anxiety, and so he ate, even though he felt too tired to do anything but sit there. Yet once he had eaten he felt less faded. He looked at his brother.

'I could hardly believe it was your voice when I heard you calling out while we were trapped in the cellar. I imagined it so many times . . .'

'I was hurrying even before the stones fell,' Zluty explained. 'I saw some blue berries last time I was in the forest and I wanted to see if they would give a blue dye. Of course, when the stones fell, I didn't bother with them. I was so anxious that you had been hurt I set the tree sap taps as soon as I arrived to let me leave a whole day sooner. But then the stones started coming down and I could not get back to the cave . . .'

'I'm sorry,' Bily said, for tears had started falling without him even knowing he would cry, and he did not seem to be able to stop them.

Zluty came at once to sit by his brother and put his arm about his shoulders.

'Our lovely cottage, Zluty,' Bily sobbed. 'I can't bear that it is ruined.'

'We will build it again,' Zluty said stoutly,
though his heart quailed at the amount of work it
would take. They had built the cottage over such a
long time. Each task had been small in itself, adding

to the complex whole that had been their home. To do it all again would take years and all the while there would be that horrible feeling of redoing something that they had done before, rather than of making something new.

'I will never be able to grow the garden the way it was . . .' Bily sighed.

'The birds will bring more seeds, and you can replant it. And you saved some of your seed collection, didn't you?'

Bily nodded wanly. 'But so much else was lost. Most of the flour and rice got wet. And what about the lovely chairs and tables you made and all the plates and cups that were broken. Oh, Zluty, how are we to live while we rebuild and replant and remake things? And what about Winter . . .'

Zluty had no answer for that. Yet Winter must be thought about, Bily knew.

'Tell me about finding the monster,' Zluty asked, giving them both another plate of mushrooms.

'At first there was a great crash. That was the monster breaking into the cellar, only I did not know it then,' Bily said.

His grey eyes lost their haunted, frightened look as he told Zluty how he had gone down into the cellar only to see the monster's eyes staring at him. Zluty listened with horror even though he knew it had not eaten Bily. It was the first time Bily had ever had such an exciting tale to tell his adventurous brother, and he was surprised how much he enjoyed it.

Then Zluty told the story of his journey and it was Bily's turn to be enthralled as he heard about the bee Queen and marvelled over her foretellings, though his face fell when Zluty spoke of the vale of bellflowers, for the delicate blooms had been destroyed along with all of the other flowers in the garden. He would have liked to speak to the bees, but they were still deeply asleep in their jar.

Zluty went on to tell about the wall he had found as he explored while trapped in the forest by the falling stones. He described the great metal egg he had found in the burned place and Bily shivered when Zluty described the white bones he had seen by the light of the shining stone. Finally he brought out the little metal egg he had found.

Bily took it and held it reverently, wondering if there was really some tiny creature inside it. He had never seen another egg like the one they had come from before, and it was very strange to think that great and small things might come from the same sort of egg.

At last Zluty told of the rain and of the diggers with their flooded burrow. Bily smiled at the image of them sitting about the fire, entranced, while outside the rain fell and fell. But when Zluty got to the part where he had looked down at the cottage, he broke off suddenly to ask Bily if the monster had said where it came from.

'It came from the West, like the red wind,' Bily said. 'It told me its people call it the *arosh*.'

'Its people,' Zluty echoed, knitting his brow. 'There are more of its kind?'

'It didn't talk much about them,' Bily said thoughtfully. 'It said it was alone in the desert when the storm came and it had to run.'

'What is a desert?' Zluty asked.

'I am not sure but the monster said nothing can live or grow there because there is no water. Not a single spring. Beyond the desert is something called mountains. I think that is where the monster lived.'

'Why did it go to a place where nothing grows or lives?'

'It said it went there to decide something,' Bily said. He glanced back down the hill in the direction of the ruins where the monster lay sleeping, watched over by Redwing, who seemed to have taken a particular liking to it. 'It is very weak. We must take care of it.'

Zluty said nothing.

'You must be very tired travelling so far,' Bily murmured after a little while. 'Sleep and we can talk more in the morning. I will keep the fire alight.'

'What about you?' Zluty asked.

'I am not tired, and when I am, I will bank the fire down and sleep,' Bily promised. Zluty nodded and stretched out with a sigh, closing his eyes. That he did not argue told Bily how exhausted he truly was. 'Everything will be all right, now that we are together,' Bily added softly. But Zluty was already sound asleep.

Instead of getting sleepier, Bily became gradually more and more wide-awake as the moon tracked across the sky. He sat cradling the small egg and thinking about Zluty's adventures. Finally, he pushed the little metal egg back into his brother's pack next to the bee jar and searched for a comb to groom his filthy tangled fur.

Zluty had said nothing of it yet, but Bily knew very well that there was a dangerous and precarious

time ahead for them. They must begin work immediately on the morrow. They would first need to
bring out everything that could be rescued from
the cellar and the ruins of the cottage. They would

dry out what could be dried out and repair what could be repaired. It was too late to plant anything now, and so they would have to concentrate on gathering food until the water in the cellar was absorbed and they could turn it into a Winter home. It would be a grim refuge but it was the only possibility of Winter shelter for it was far too late to build even the smallest cottage in the time that remained before Winter. They would both need to spend all of their time foraging for food if they were to have enough to survive until Spring.

Bily might even have to do some of the journeying that Zluty had always done before, if Zluty was right about the wild crops being damaged. But after all that had happened to Bily since the red wind had come, this no longer seemed such a terrifying prospect.

He set aside the comb and took the pot of heated water and a rug down to the monster in the hope that its fever might finally have broken.

He was quite close to it before he realised that the monster's great bright eyes were open.

'Are you in pain?' he asked it gently.

'I am thirsty . . .' the monster said in its thick rough voice.

Bily lifted the bowl of water and held it so that the monster could lap from it. When it had drunk its fill, he set the bowl down and offered food.

'I am not hungry,' it said.

'You ought to try to eat anyway,' Bily told it. 'You will never regain your strength otherwise.'

'I fear that food will not give me back my strength,' said the monster.

There was a grim note in its voice that made Bily feel uneasy. 'It is only a matter of time before your strength returns,' he said.

The monster's eyes, which had turned to the West, now returned to him, and there was sadness in them. 'I wish that were so, my little friend, I truly do. But I fear that I have finally come to the bad end that was always foretold for those who shirk their duty.'

'I am sure you did what you were supposed to do,' Bily said stoutly.

'There are many kinds of duties,' murmured the monster with a sigh. Again its eyes turned to the West. 'There was a . . . thing I was meant to be given. I did not want it and that was why I was in the desert. In truth, I was so busy trying to come up with reasons why I ought not to have what I was to be given, that I did not see the signs of the stone storm. Some of my people say that the *arosh* comes only when change is needed. Others say it comes to destroy what is unworthy. Maybe it came to drive me away . . .'

'Are you so important, Monster, that a whole wind would rise and gather up stones just to stop you from having something that you did not want in the first place?' Bily asked, laughing a little.

The monster looked at him for a long moment, and then a flicker of humour came into its eyes. 'You are right, small one. I am not so important. It is good to be reminded of that.'

'What happened to you was an accident,' Bily said firmly. 'And when you have healed, you can simply go back and get whatever it was you were supposed to have. In the meantime, I will take care of you.'

The monster made no comment and Bily removed the bandage and set about bathing its paw. He was elated to see that some of the redness had faded, as well as the swelling. 'I think the honey helped,' he said.

'Among my people, there is not much kindness to creatures of different kinds,' said the monster thoughtfully, and his eyes flickered to Redwing, who was perched on the edge of the fragment of metal egg, watching them with her bright eyes. The monster turned back to Bily. 'You saved my life. I will not forget it.'

The monster looked away again and Bily followed its gaze. It was looking at the little glow of the campfire Zluty had made. 'I should like to hear more about this Northern Forest your brother visited. There are tales of a forest told among my people, but I had never imagined it was a real place.'

'You must ask him to tell you the story of his journey,' Bily said eagerly. 'But now I will go and bring you some food. You need to eat a little and then you should sleep.'

'Thank you,' said the monster.

Bily understood from its grave tone that he was being thanked for more than his advice and his offer of food, and he felt himself blush as he hurried away.

16

Zluty woke just before dawn feeling very stiff. He opened his eyes and saw Bily lying sound asleep, his cheeks pink from the ruddy glow of the embers of the dying fire. Despite all that he had endured in the last few days, Bily's face was serene in sleep and Zluty felt a rush of love for his brother. He must have spent hours grooming himself the night before, because his fur was as white and soft as ever.

Zluty got out of his bed and padded away from the fire to give himself a good brush. Then he gathered some more ground cones and crept back

to build up the fire, trying to be quiet so that he
would not wake Bily. The bees were awake and the
three males flew out of their jar to accompany him
when he walked down to the pool of water beside

the cottage. It was a murky colour but it smelled clean enough for him to wash his face in. It was definitely deeper than it had been and he thought of what Bily had told him about the crack in the floor of the cellar cave, and the water rushing in even after the rain had stopped. The combination of the stone storm and the heavy rain must have changed the ground so that what had been a trickle of water from deep underground had increased to a strong gush with more than one outlet.

If he was right, there could be no hope of rebuilding the old cottage. They would have to build a new one on higher ground. For now, the best they could do for a shelter was to use the stones from the broken wall to make a small hut. The bits of the old egg house in the cellar would have to serve as a roof. It would have to be a very small hut though, because they would need to spend every moment gathering supplies for the coming Winter.

Zluty decided that since he was awake he might as well start bringing up anything that could be salvaged from the cellar. He did not like the idea of getting wet again, especially when he had just combed himself, but it would have to be done sooner or later and at least there was now a fire waiting to warm him.

He climbed over the broken wall and found himself right alongside the pallet where the monster slept. It was panting slightly and Zluty wondered if it was thirsty. He took up the bowl on the ground, only to find there was water in it.

Suddenly the monster woke and reared up to snarl terrifyingly at him, showing all of its sharp teeth.

Zluty's fur fluffed with fright, but already the monster was sinking back.

'So it was not a dream,' it rasped.

Zluty swallowed hard, thinking how much bigger it appeared in the daylight. He told himself that it only looked that way because its long thick fur had dried and fluffed out. But it was not only its size that daunted him. The monster had long sharp claws and pointed white teeth. Even its ears were sharply pointed. Everything about it looked dangerous. The previous night when they had brought it out of the cellar, it had looked so ill and feverish that Zluty had felt sure it would not wake again. But the eyes fixed upon him now were bright with life and intelligence, and he was within easy reach of its paws if it had recovered enough to use them.

'I am sorry if I frightened you,' said the monster gravely.

Zluty swallowed and said as firmly as he could, 'Are you hungry? I can get you some food.'

The monster said, 'I am thirsty.'

Zluty was steeling himself to step nearer to the pallet when Bily touched him on the shoulder. Zluty got such a fright he dropped the bowl, which crashed to the ground and shattered.

'Oh no!' he groaned, for it was a bowl that his brother had spent hours colouring delicately with strokes of a feather.

'Never mind,' Bily said. 'So much has been smashed that one more thing hardly matters.'

Zluty stared at his brother in disbelief, for Bily had always set great store on the things he made. He had sometimes even wept when something he particularly liked broke in the firing kiln.

Zluty said, 'The . . . the monster was thirsty.'

'That is a good sign,' Bily approved. 'Its fever broke last night.' He bent down and carefully picked up a broken piece of the bowl that still held water. Zluty watched as he brought it to the monster, marvelling at Bily's fearlessness as it drank. When it lifted its head, licking drops of water from its muzzle with its long red tongue, Zluty swallowed hard.

'You needn't be afraid,' Bily said, to Zluty's mortification, setting the broken bowl down carefully. 'If it was going to eat me it could easily have done it by now.'

'Right now I am so weak that your bird friend could land on my nose and pull my whiskers out and I could not lift a paw to stop her,' said the monster.

Zluty blushed but was secretly rather relieved to hear this. He said nothing as he watched Bily examine the blackclaw bite. The monster only winced.

'It looks much better,' Bily murmured.

'It is still very sore,' said the monster through gritted teeth.

Bily ignored this and went back to the fire to get some warm water to bathe the paw again. Zluty remained with the monster, but neither spoke. When Bily returned, he had brought a bowl of cold mushrooms as well as the water. He set the food down where the monster could reach it and began to wash the paw, saying, 'It had better be left uncovered from now on. The air will dry it and the sun will be good for it, but you must move it as little as possible.'

'You sound exactly like a seer,' grumbled the monster.

'What is a seer?' Zluty asked curiously.

'One among my people who sees things others do not,' said the monster. 'So it is said.'

'What do you mean by "your people"?' Zluty asked curiously.

'I mean those like me. My kind. My brothers and sisters and my mother and father and my cousins and uncles but also those that are not of my blood,' answered the monster.

'I do not know what any of those other things are, other than brother,' said Zluty.

'You have no family?' asked the monster. 'There have been times when I have wished it so for myself. But tell me, why do you and your brother choose to live apart from your kind?'

'There are no others of our kind,' Zluty said.

The monster stared at him. 'Something cannot come from nothing. You must have had a mother and father.'

'We came from an egg,' Zluty said.

'You both came from the same egg?'

'Of course,' said Bily, who had finished with the paw. 'Sometimes two birds are born from the same egg.'

'But you are not birds,' said the monster.

'Of course not,' Bily said. 'But birds are not the only things born out of eggs. The dusk lizard comes out of an egg, too.'

'A bird or a lizard lays the egg from which a bird or a lizard is born,' said the monster. 'Where is the She that laid your egg?'

Bily and Zluty looked at one another, for it was not a thing they had ever thought about before. Bily said slowly, 'I suppose the egg was laid and then whatever laid it left, just as the dusk lizard lays her eggs in the earth and covers them over before leaving.'

The monster opened its mouth, but before it could speak a fit of coughing overtook it.

Bily tut-tutted and drew its blankets over it. 'You must eat and then rest.'

The monster lay down its great head, and when its eyes closed Bily and Zluty exchanged a look. For the first time, Zluty felt some of the pity that his brother felt for the monster, for clearly it was still very weak.

Several peaceful though oddly makeshift days followed during which the water in the black pool and the cellar did not recede, though neither did it deepen. Zluty wondered if he was wrong about the spring. Maybe the cracks in the ground were closing up and the waters would recede after some time. Then they could rebuild their old cottage in the Spring.

Bily and Zluty began to raise the beginnings of a second wall, for Zluty had pointed out that even if the cellar did eventually drain, it would not do so in time to be used as a shelter for the Winter.

Little by little they brought out all that could be salvaged from the cellar, but to Billy's disappointment, they had not yet managed to find his precious spindle. Fortunately, they had been able to get the water jugs out because the water in the pool was beginning to grow stagnant.

This puzzled Zluty, for surely spring water was flowing into it through the submerged well, and ought to be refreshing it. The only answer seemed to be that there was something in the stones that had fallen into the well that was fouling it. In time, he was sure the spring would recover, but until then the water in the jugs was all they had besides the pool in the cave by the Northern Forest. Of course, the diggers would always trade diggermilk for food. But food was soon likely to be another problem.

One day, Zluty left Bily laying out his seeds to dry in the hope that some might be salvaged,

and walked a half day East to look at the patch of
sweetgrass he usually harvested for new bedding.
The crop had been so completely destroyed by the
stonefall that it might never have existed.

The next day he went further East to dig for
orange tubers, having warned Bily that he would

not return until the following day. He managed to locate a few roots, but they smelled strongly of the red stones, and Redwing and the other birds had refused utterly to eat anything that smelled of them, explaining that it would make them sick.

Two days later, Zluty went South to the swamp. He had been afraid that the wild rice would also be tainted by the red stones, but the swamp had swollen to many times its size, drowning not only the openings to the blackclaw nests but all the wild rice.

Zluty was very glad when he came across a tuft of bright yellow flowers of a kind he had never seen before on the way back. Wild flowers often grew on ledges in the rifts after rain, and although their smell told Zluty the flowers were inedible, he knew Bily would enjoy their colour and perhaps the bees would be able to harvest the pollen. It was much better not to go back empty-handed, given his bad news.

Bily had exclaimed in pleasure at the sight of the flowers, and the bees emerged from their jar to swoop on them at once. But when Zluty told him about the swamp, Bily's face fell. He knew as well as Zluty that even with all that his brother had

brought back from his trip to the Northern Forest, there was too little they had managed to salvage from the cellar storage to last them the whole Winter without the wild crops.

Bily might have worried more if the monster's cough had not that afternoon turned into a severe chill. The monster shivered and shook the whole evening, and though Bily tended to it constantly, replacing the blankets that kept falling off, and feeding it warmed honey water that Zluty brought down from the fire, it was worse by nightfall. The monster was so painfully thin now that its bones showed through its skin, and looking at it, Zluty could not help but wondering if it would not have been better for it to die swiftly like the diggers, rather than to linger on in this dreadful way.

But he said nothing of that to Bily whose heart was set on saving the monster.

Nor did he say that, even if the monster did survive, they were all likely to die of thirst or hunger before the Winter was out. He had a habit of protecting his gentle brother, but after he helped Bily drag his mattress down to flat ground so that they could pull the pallet out of the ruins and he could sleep by the monster, Zluty sat on the broken stone wall reflecting that, for the first time in his life, he did not know what to do next.

17

The next morning, Bily woke to hear the monster speaking.

'You will die if you go North,' it said in its soft thick voice, wheezing only a little.

Before Bily could sit up and ask what it meant, he heard Zluty speak.

'How did you know what I was thinking?' he asked, sounding wary.

Bily kept his eyes shut, listening.

The monster gave a heavy sigh. 'There are those among my people who see more than others. Seers they are called. I have told you of them. But there are others besides them who have the power to see things that have yet to come. It seems I am one of them, though I never knew it until the *arosh* chased me over the desert. Just now I felt you would convince Bily to go to the Northern Forest for the Winter. But if you do that, you will both die.'

'I have been there many times without harm,' Zluty said. 'There is water and a cave we can shelter in, and abundant food in the forest.'

'You have never been there in the Winter when meat-eating beasts come to take shelter and find water, just as you would do,' answered the monster.

A shiver of fear ran down Bily's spine.

'I have seen no sign of such beasts,' protested Zluty. 'How do you know beasts come there? You have never been there.'

'No, but I think this Northern Forest of yours is one that my people tell about. And the stories are full of fell Winter beasts that are drawn there when the cold comes to prey upon the small creatures that dwell there.'

'If we stay here we will die,' Zluty said in a low voice. 'The water is foul and the wild crops are all dead. We do not have food enough to last the Winter.'

'That is true,' said the monster. 'If you would live, you must travel to the West. You must leave very soon if you would survive, for you will have to cross the desert and the mountains before the Winter comes.'

There was a silence and then Zluty said, 'The bee Queen told me that she had seen me bringing the little queen to the vale of bellflowers. I thought she meant the cottage, but she made the bees put a lot of honey into the pot for the journey.'

'You should leave today,' said the monster.

'We can't go so soon,' Zluty protested. 'We must make preparations and you are too weak to travel safely.'

'You must leave me behind,' the monster answered.

'No!' said Bily, springing up and glaring at them both. 'If we have to go away, we are all going together.'

'I cannot walk, Little One,' said the monster gently. 'The blackclaw poison did not kill me, but it has weakened me badly. I may never be able to walk again.'

'We can pull you in the pallet,' Bily said. 'And if we go West, eventually we will come to your people. They will know how to help you.'

The monster stared at him. 'You would move too slowly, and you would need more water and food for three than for two.'

'I'm not leaving without you,' Bily said.

The monster sighed and turned its eyes to Zluty. 'You must make your brother understand that this is impossible.'

Zluty sighed. 'I'm sorry, Monster, but if Bily is determined that we must take you, we don't have any choice, for he is terribly stubborn. Besides, if we go West, as you say we must, it is unknown terrain for us. It may be that we will not survive without your knowledge.'

'Oh, Zluty!' Bily cried, and flung his arms around his brother and hugged him tightly.

'If you both perish trying to save me, I will have repaid you ill for saving my life,' said the monster.

'If we leave you, I will not have saved your life,' Bily said, sounding elated.

'We can tie all of the food we have saved and the water urns to the pallet, and I can rig up a canopy to make a sort of roof over it,' Zluty said thoughtfully.

'I will make some pancakes for us to take with us, and we will need to take as many ground cones as we can for fire, if the desert is as bare as the monster told me,' Bily said decidedly.

The monster sighed. 'This is foolishness.'

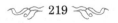

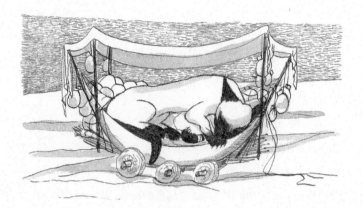

By dusk, Bily had finished fussing and rearranging packages about the sides of the wheeled pallet and he went to say goodbye to the diggers and to make them a gift of all the food and the white fluffs he had dried out, which they could not take with them. The diggers would survive well enough for they always had a great deal of food stored away and they would certainly have enough to last for the Winter to come with what he was giving them. Whether or not they would find the world restored by Spring, he did not know, but he hoped for their sake that the taint left by the red stones would fade so that the wild crops would grow again. Some of his flowers might even reseed in time, and it gave Bily a queer feeling to imagine flowers blooming beside the empty ruin of their cottage.

Zluty took the opportunity to force himself to go into the cellar one last time to see if he could find Bily's spindle. There was only one corner of the cellar he had yet to search, and the water stank badly, but he took a deep breath and ducked under, feeling about with both hands. He was about to give up after going under for the third time, when he found it.

He bore his prize up to the sunlight triumphantly and shook himself dry before setting about cleaning it with a twist of sweetgrass.

'You know this is madness,' the monster said to him. 'Why did you agree?'

'I know that Bily would never forgive himself if he left you,' Zluty said softly. 'The truth is that I am glad he is so determined to save you. I do not think he would have been able to bear leaving the cottage otherwise.'

The monster gave him a curious look. 'You underestimate your brother.'

'I know that he will be braver for your sake than for his own,' Zluty said.

Both fell silent when Bily returned and Zluty presented him with the spindle.

'It is strange,' Bily said, glancing up at the few remaining stars as they got up the following morning. 'I have lain awake so many nights worrying before you made your journeys, and yet now that I am going with you I find I am not anxious for either of us. I am only sad that we must leave the cottage.

'We could come back, after the Winter ends,' Zluty said, thinking how lonely it would be to journey with no image of home and a lantern in a window to draw him on. But then he looked at Bily, and his heart grew calm, for it was his brother that had made the cottage a home.

'We won't ever come back here,' Bily said softly. He heaved a sigh and stood up. 'Let us go. It is better to be gone than going.'

'It is not too late to leave me,' said the monster, as Zluty tied their bedding to the pallet.

In answer, Bily took up one of the ropes fastened at the front of the pallet and Zluty took the other. The brothers smiled at one another and, without a word, they turned to face West, and began their journey.

Overhead, Redwing swooped and soared, piping her joy, for unknown to all of them, she was going home.

Also by Isobelle Carmody

The second book in The Kingdom of the Lost series.

Adventure and danger follow Bily, Zluty, Redwing and the
Monster as they cross a desert and journey through high stony
mountains in search of a new home.

A magical series for younger readers from the award-winning
author of *Little Fur*.

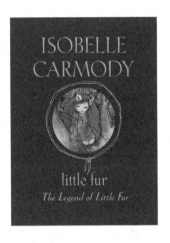

ISOBELLE
CARMODY

little fur
The Legend of Little Fur

Little Fur is an elf troll who lives in a secret wilderness
at the heart of a great human city. She is a healer.
She sings to the ancient trees that protect
the small wilderness.

But one day Crow tells of humans who will come to burn
the trees. To protect her home and her friends,
Little Fur must venture for the first time into the dangerous
human world . . .

Little Fur has battled once before with those who would
destroy the great earth spirit that nurtures all living things.
Now her fate becomes entangled with the mysterious fox,
Sorrow, and together they must travel to Underth
in a dangerous quest to uncover the evil plans of the troll king.

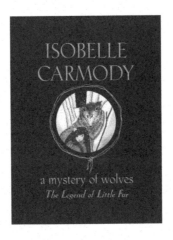

ISOBELLE
CARMODY

a mystery of wolves
The Legend of Little Fur

Discovering that her friend Ginger is in terrible danger,
Little Fur frees the old wolf Greysong from the zoo and
together they travel to the frozen mountains. There she must
face the deadly peril that lies at the heart of the Mystery of
Wolves, and learn about her own mysterious past.

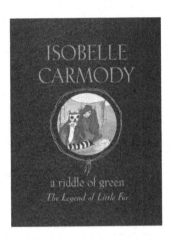

ISOBELLE
CARMODY

a riddle of green
The Legend of Little Fur

All her life, Little Fur has healed others. This time, it is she
who needs healing. Beginning a strange and dangerous journey
that will take her far from her beloved wilderness,
Little Fur seeks out the earth spirit that links all living things.
Will she find it in time?

About the Author

Isobelle Carmody began the first of her highly acclaimed Obernewtyn Chronicles while she was still at high school, and worked on the series while completing university. The series, and her many award-winning short stories and books for young people, have established her at the forefront of fantasy writing in Australia and overseas.

Little Fur, Isobelle's first series for younger readers, won the 2006 ABPA Design Awards. *The Red Wind* was awarded the 2011 CBC Book of the Year Award for Younger Readers.

Isobelle divides her time between her home on the Great Ocean Road in Australia and her travels abroad.

Acknowledgements

Thanks first and foremost to my editor Katrina, and her little inner traveller, for sharing the journey; to Jan and to my brother Ken, whose generous artistic advice and suggestions were invaluable; to Marina, for her wonderful design skills and patience with me; and to John and Virginia for inviting me to share their sanctuary on Santorini Island, where I wrote *The Red Wind*.